"Food always tastes better eaten outside."

He glanced around the park, noting that several other families had taken advantage of the picnic tables. "Oh, I don't know," he mused, thinking of ants and flies and a host of other associated nuisances, not to mention spilled drinks and sticky hands. "It isn't always a great experience."

She chuckled. "Let me guess. Your idea of eating outside is gobbling down a bagel or a burger while you're stuck in traffic."

It was uncanny how accurately she could read him—and they'd hardly spent any time together. How much of his soul would she see by the end of two months? "Yeah," he admitted.

"That doesn't count. You have to soak up the ambience of your surroundings. Allow nature's scents of pine and honeysuckle and lavender to mingle with the aroma of the food." She inhaled. "That's what dining outdoors is all about."

As she closed her eyes he had the strangest urge to trace the line of her jaw with his fingertips. He also wanted to see if her strawberry-blond hair was as soft as it looked, to discover if she'd fit against his body as perfectly as he imagined.

Giving in to temptation wasn't a wise thing to do. He simply had to deny that sudden attraction—because if he didn't it would only create more problems in the long run. They were only two people who shared the responsibility of two kids for a few months. Nothing more, nothing less.

And yet her soft skin beckoned…

Dear Reader

I've always wanted to write a cancer survivor story because so many of us have had our lives touched by this disease, whether from personal experience or through the experience of a friend or family member. Finally I sensed it was time to tell the story that had been waiting patiently for its turn.

Facing a life-threatening disease takes a lot of courage, and that became the main character trait of my heroine, Christy. Her courage, however, comes at a high price, which means she needs a hero who will be strong when she needs strength, compassionate when she needs compassion, and dependable when she needs someone to depend on. Linc is her perfect partner—although Christy has a difficult time believing...

Fortunately, love conquers all. I hope you enjoy being a part of Christy and Linc's journey as they search for and find their own happy ending.

Until next time

Jessica

UNLOCKING THE SURGEON'S HEART

BY
JESSICA MATTHEWS

First published in Great Britain 2012
by Mills & Boon, an imprint of Harlequin (UK) Limited.
Large Print edition 2012
Harlequin (UK) Limited, Eton House,
18-24 Paradise Road, Richmond, Surrey TW9 1SR

© Jessica Matthews 2012

ISBN: 978 0 263 22491 7

Harlequin (UK) policy is to use papers that are
natural, renewable and recyclable products and made
from wood grown in sustainable forests. The logging
and manufacturing process conform to the legal
environmental regulations of the country of origin.

Printed and bound in Great Britain
by CPI Antony Rowe, Chippenham, Wiltshire

Jessica Matthews's interest in medicine began at a young age, and she nourished it with medical stories and hospital-based television programmes. After a stint as a teenage candy-striper, she pursued a career as a clinical laboratory scientist. When not writing or on duty, she fills her day with countless family and school-related activities. Jessica lives in the central United States, with her husband, daughter and son.

Recent titles by the same author:

THE CHILD WHO RESCUED CHRISTMAS
MAVERICK IN THE ER
SIX-WEEK MARRIAGE MIRACLE
EMERGENCY: PARENTS NEEDED
HIS BABY BOMBSHELL
THE BABY DOCTOR'S BRIDE

**These books are also available
in eBook format
from www.millsandboon.co.uk**

This book is dedicated to cancer survivors
everywhere—especially my friend
Carla Maneth, who so graciously
shared her experiences and insights—
and to the memory of those who fought hard
but didn't win the battle—
especially my mother and my father-in-law.

CHAPTER ONE

IT WAS a shame, really. A man as handsome as Lincoln Maguire should have a personality to match, shouldn't he? The good doctor—and he was more than good, he was *exceptional* when it came to his surgical expertise—was so completely focused on his work that he wouldn't recognize a light-hearted moment if one landed in the middle of his operating field.

Christy Michaels peered sideways at the man in question. His long, lean fingers danced across the keyboard as he clearly ignored the hospital staff's ideas and opinions regarding Mercy Memorial's part in Levitt Springs' upcoming Community Harvest Festival. Apparently, talk of craft booths, food vendors, and a golf tournament to benefit the cancer center and the local Relay for Life chapter didn't interest him enough to join in the conversation.

It wasn't the first time he'd distanced himself

from the conversations swirling around him; he was the sort who came in, saw his patients, and left, usually with few people being the wiser. Today, though, his distant demeanor—as if these details were too unimportant for his notice—coupled with her own special interest in the center and the treatment it provided, irritated her.

"I have an idea," she blurted out, well aware that she didn't but it hadn't been for lack of trying. She'd been considering options—and discarding them—for weeks, because none had given her that inner assurance that "this was the one".

Yet as voices stilled and all eyes focused on her—except for one midnight-blue pair—she had to come up with something unusual, something noteworthy enough to shock Dr Maguire into paying attention. With luck, he might even come out of his own little world and get involved.

"Make it snappy, Michaels," Denise Danton, her shift manager, said as she glanced at her watch. "The festival committee meets in five minutes and it takes at least that long to walk to the conference room."

Acknowledging Denise with a brief nod, she began, "It's something we haven't done before."

One of the nurses groaned. "If you're going to

suggest a bachelor auction, it's already been mentioned. Personally, I think we need a newer idea."

Darn it, but that *had* been her suggestion. Rather than admit defeat, she thought fast. "We could create our own version of *Dancing with the Stars.* Only we would call it *Dancing with the Doctors.*"

Instantly, his hands slowed, and she was immensely pleased. And yet he didn't look away from the digital pages in front of him, so maybe he was only thinking about Mrs Halliday's chest tube and her antibiotic regimen.

"How would that work?" someone asked her.

She ad-libbed. "We'd sell tickets for the public to watch the doctors and their partners perform. People could vote for their favorite pair—making a donation for the privilege, of course—and at the end, one lucky team is crowned the winner and all proceeds benefit the hospital."

Denise looked thoughtful. "Oh, I like that. We'd have to strong-arm enough physicians to participate, though."

"I'm sure any of them would jump at the opportunity to raise money for a good cause. Right, Dr Maguire?" she asked innocently.

If she hadn't taken that moment to glance directly at the side of his face, she might have missed the weary set to his mouth as well as the barely imperceptible shadow on his skin that suggested his day had begun far earlier than hers. The wisps of walnut-brown hair appearing out from under his green cap were damp, and perspiration dotted the bridge of his chiseled nose. His scrub suit was wrinkled and his breast pocket had a frayed edge at the seam.

Funny thing, but she hadn't noticed he'd looked quite so frazzled when he'd sat in the chair.

Instantly, Christy felt guilty for distracting him. In hindsight, she realized it wasn't his scheduled surgery day, which meant he was obviously filling in for one of his partners. It also meant he was rushing to finish the paperwork so he could see his private patients. From the volume of cases he brought to the hospital, his waiting room was probably packed and growing more so by the minute.

"Sure, why not," he answered without any real emotion, his attention still focused on his computer screen.

"Okay, then," she said brightly, ready to leave him to his work. "Denise, you can mention this at your meeting—"

"Dr Maguire," the other woman said boldly, "you wouldn't mind participating, would you?"

This time, his hands froze. To Christy's surprise and dismay, his dark blue gaze met hers instead of Denise's and she was sure she saw exasperation in those depths. He clearly held her responsible, not only for being interrupted but also for having to field Denise's request.

However, when he addressed Denise, his tone was as pleasant and even-tempered as ever. "I'll forego the spot to make room for someone who's more capable."

"Ability has nothing to do with it," Denise retorted. "This is all for fun and as Christy said, it's for a good cause."

"But—" he began.

"If you sign up, I just *know* more of the medical staff will be willing to join in," Denise coaxed. "And with you on the program, we'll sell tons of tickets. Just think how much we'll earn for the cancer center."

Christy groaned inwardly. He *would* be a big draw because she couldn't imagine anyone who wouldn't be willing to fork out money to see the straitlaced, cool, and collected Lincoln Maguire cut loose on the dance floor. More importantly, because it was a known fact that he didn't date, everyone would want to speculate about the lucky woman he'd chosen to be his partner.

His thoughts obviously ran along the same track because he shot a warning glare in her direction before he spoke to Denise. "You're giving me far too much credit—"

"Nonsense." She clapped her hands softly in her excitement. "This is going to be great. The committee will love this idea. I can't wait to tell them—"

"Stop right there," he ordered in his most authoritative voice.

No one moved. Christy didn't even breathe because she suddenly had a feeling of impending doom as he pinned her with his gaze.

"If you're penciling me on the list," he said firmly, "I have a couple of conditions. One, if you have more volunteers than you can accommodate, my name will be the first to be removed."

Denise frowned, but, apparently recognizing his tone brooked no argument, she nodded. "Okay. Not a problem."

"Second, in the event that doesn't happen—and I suspect someone will make sure that it doesn't," he added dryly, "Christy must agree to be my partner."

Everyone's heads turned toward her in a perfectly choreographed motion. Expressions ranged from surprise to curiosity and a few were also speculative.

"You want…what?" Christy asked hoarsely. He might be her best friend's brother-in-law, but that wasn't a solid connection to warrant such a request. After all, they'd only been at Gail and Tyler's house together on two occasions and they'd hardly spoken to each other.

"To be my partner."

This wasn't supposed to happen. "Why me?" she asked.

He raised an eyebrow. "This was your idea," he reminded her. "It's only fair that you participate, too."

He had a point, although if she had her choice, she'd pick someone who complemented her, not someone who was vinegar to her oil. While in the hospital they'd dealt with each other amicably over the past two years—he gave orders and she carried them out—but in the private atmosphere of Gail's home their differences had been highlighted. As a man who prided himself on control and self-restraint, she'd seen how he didn't appreciate her outspoken and sometimes impulsive nature.

Neither would she delude herself into believing he'd set his condition with romantic motives in mind. According to Gail, her brother-in-law had mapped out his life so carefully that he wasn't allowing for a wife until he was forty, and as he still had two or three years until then, his work was his mistress.

"Unless, of course, you object," he added smoothly, if not a trifle smugly, as if he *expected* her to refuse so she could provide his get-out-of-jail-free card.

She didn't blame him for thinking that. It was no secret she wasn't interested in a romance any more than he was, but while his excuse was because his work consumed his life, her reasons were entirely different.

However, he'd issued a challenge and she was living proof that she didn't back down from one. If dusting off her dancing shoes and practicing her two-step meant the workaholic, type A personality Dr Maguire would participate in a night of fun and frivolity, then she'd do it.

She shrugged. "Okay, fine with me."

"Good," Denise said. "It's settled."

"I don't know how settled this is." He sounded doubtful and hopeful at the same time. "Won't the committee, as a whole, have to approve the idea first?"

"Trust me, they're going to love the concept," the older woman assured him. "I can already think of fifty ways to promote the event and guarantee a brilliant turnout. Now, I'm off. Hold the fort while I'm gone, people, so that means everyone back to work!"

The crowd dispersed, but Christy hardly noticed. Dr Maguire—Linc, as Gail affectionately called him—sat in his chair, arms crossed, as he drilled her with his gaze.

A weaker woman would have quaked under his piercing stare, but she'd stared death in the face and Linc Maguire wasn't nearly as intimidating. Still, she felt a little uncomfortable as she waited for him to speak. From the way he worked his jaw and frowned periodically, he obviously had trouble verbalizing his thoughts.

"*Dancing with the Doctors*?" he finally asked, his expression so incredulous she wanted to laugh, but knew she shouldn't. "Was that the best you could do?"

She shrugged, relieved that he seemed more stunned than angry, at least at this point. "On short notice, yes. However, from everyone's response, the idea was a hit."

"It was something all right," he grumbled. "If I were you, I'd pray the committee thinks it's ridiculous and dreams up another plan."

"I don't think *Dancing with the Docs* is so bad," she protested. "You have to admit the concept is unusual. We've never done anything like this before."

"We haven't had an old-fashioned box supper or a kissing booth either," he pointed out. "It doesn't mean we should start now."

Unbidden, her gaze landed on his mouth. To her, it was perfect with the bottom lip just a little wider than the top. No doubt there was a host of other women who'd agree.

Oddly enough, it only seemed natural for her gaze to travel lower, down his neck to a sculpted chest that even the shapeless scrub top and white undershirt didn't disguise. His skin was tan, and dark hair covered his muscular arms, indicating that somewhere in his busy schedule he found time to work out on a regular basis.

Oh, my. And she was going to be in his arms,

pressed against that chest, in front of hundreds of people? Maybe she *should* start praying the committee wouldn't be interested in her idea. Better yet, she could pray for enough physicians to volunteer so the team of Maguire and Michaels would be excused from the lineup.

She swallowed hard. "It's for a good cause," she said lamely.

"Tell yourself that when you're nursing a few broken toes," he mumbled darkly.

His expression reminded her more of a sullen little boy than a confident surgeon and it made her chuckle. "You don't dance?"

He shook his head. "Other than a slow shuffle? No."

She wasn't surprised. In her view, Lincoln Maguire was too controlled and tightly wound to ever do anything as uninhibited as gliding around a dance floor in step to the music. However, she was curious about his reasons.

"You surely practiced a few steps for your senior prom, didn't you?"

He blinked once, as if she'd caught him off guard. "I didn't go. The girl I'd asked turned me down."

Remorse hit her again. She hadn't intended

to embarrass him, or trigger bad memories. "I'm sorry."

"I'm not," he said, matter-of-factly. "We were just good friends and she was waiting for a buddy of mine to dredge up the courage to ask her himself. As soon as I knew her feelings leaned in his direction, I told him and the rest, as they say, is history. In fact, they celebrated their twelve-year anniversary this year."

"Talk about being versatile," she teased. "You're a surgeon *and* a matchmaker."

He grinned. "Don't be too impressed. They were the first and only couple I pushed together."

She was too caught up by the transformation his smile had caused to be embarrassed by her remark. He looked younger than his thirty-seven years and appeared far more approachable. His chiseled-from-granite features softened and he seemed more hot-blooded male than cold-hearted surgeon.

His smile was also too infectious for her not to return it in full measure. However, if she told anyone he had actually softened enough to smile, they'd never believe her.

Neither would anyone believe her if she told

them they'd actually discussed something *personal* instead of a patient. As far as she knew, it was the first time such a thing had happened in the history of the hospital.

"I hate to break this to you," she said, "but a slow shuffle won't cut it when it comes to a competition."

"Only if your *Dancing with the Doctors* idea takes hold," he pointed out. "With luck, it won't and we'll both be off the hook."

She heard the hopeful note in his voice. "Trust me, the committee will love it. You may as well accept the fact you're going to dance before hundreds of people."

He frowned for several seconds before he let out a heavy sigh of resignation. "I suppose."

"And that means you're going to have to learn a few steps. A waltz, maybe even a tango or a foxtrot."

"Surely not." His face looked as pained as his voice.

"Surely so," she assured him. "It'll be fun."

He shot her a you've-got-to-be-kidding look before his Adam's apple bobbed. He'd clearly, and quite literally, found her comment hard to swallow.

"Tripping over one's feet in front of an audience isn't fun," he pointed out.

"That's why one learns," she said sweetly. "So we don't trip over our feet, or our partner's. Besides, I know you're the type who can master any skill that's important to you. Look at how well you can keyboard. Most docs are still on the hunt-and-peck method but you're in the same league as a transcriptionist."

"I'm a surgeon. I'm *supposed* to be good with my hands," he said, clearly dismissing her praise. Unbidden, her gaze dropped to the body part in question. For an instant she imagined what it would be like to enjoy this man's touch. Would he make love with the same single-minded approach he gave everything else in his life that he deemed important?

Sadly, she'd never know. She couldn't risk the rejection again. However, it had been a long time since she'd been in a relationship and he was handsome enough to make any girl dream of possibilities....

"Hands, feet, they all follow the brain's commands. 'Where there's a will there's a way'," she quoted.

He rubbed the back of his neck as he grimaced.

"Are you always full of helpful advice, Nurse Pollyanna?" he complained.

Oh, my, but she'd just experienced another first—the most taciturn physician on staff had actually *teased* her. She was going to have to look outside for snow, which never fell in the Midwest in August.

"I try." In the distance, she heard the tell-tale alarm that signaled someone's IV bag had emptied. As if the noise had suddenly reminded him of time and place, he straightened, pulled on his totally professional demeanor like a well-worn lab coat, and pointed to the monitor.

"Keep an eye on Mrs Hollings's chest tube. Call me if you notice any change."

She was strangely disappointed to see the congenial Lincoln Maguire had been replaced by his coolly polite counterpart. "Will do."

Without giving him a backward glance, she rushed to take care of John Carter's IV. He'd had a rough night after his knee-replacement surgery and now that they'd finally got his pain under control, he was catching up on his sleep. She quickly silenced the alarm, hung a fresh bag of fluid, then left the darkened room and returned to the nurses' station. To her surprise, Linc hadn't budged from his spot. He was simply sitting there…as if waiting. For her, maybe? Impossible. Yet it was a heady thought.

"One more thing," he said without preamble.

"What's that?" she asked, intending to head to the supply cabinet on his other side in order to replenish the supply of alcohol wipes she kept in her cargo pants pocket.

He rose, effectively blocking her path. "I'll pick you up tonight."

Flustered by his statement, she made the mistake of meeting his blue-black gaze, which at her five-eight required some effort because he was at least six-three. It was a gaze that exuded confidence and lingered a few seconds too long.

"Pick me up?" she said. "What for?"

"You're going to Gail and Ty's for dinner, aren't you?"

"Yes," she began cautiously, "but how did you know?"

"Because they invited me, too."

Great. The first time Gail had hosted a dinner to include both of them, it had turned into a miserable evening. It had been obvious from the way Gail had steered the conversation that she'd been trying to push them together and her efforts had backfired. Lincoln had sat through the next hour wearing the most pained expression in between checking his watch every five minutes. To make matters worse, his attitude had made her nervous, so she'd chattered nonstop until he'd finally left with clear relief on his face. After that, Gail had promised never to put either of them through the misery of a private dinner again.

While the past few minutes had been pleasant, she wasn't going to believe that *this* dinner would end differently. Given his unhappiness over the fundraising idea, the results would be the same. It was inevitable.

"How nice," she said inanely.

"So I'll swing by and get you."

She bristled under his commanding tone. He might be able to expect his orders to be obeyed at the hospital, but this was *her* private life and she made her own decisions.

"Thanks, but don't go to the trouble. I'll drive myself."

"It's not inconvenient at all. Your house is on my way."

She stared at him, incredulous. She'd always believed he barely knew who she was, but he knew where she lived? How was that possible?

"Don't look so horrified," he said impatiently, as if offended by her surprise. "Gail gave me the address and suggested we come together."

Good old Gail. Her friend simply wouldn't stop in her effort to convince her to get back in the dating game, but to use her own brother-in-law when their previous encounter had turned into such a disaster? It only showed how determined—and desperate—her happily married buddy was.

"That's sweet, but I'd rather—"

"I'll pick you up at six," he said, before he strode away, leaving her to sputter at his high-handedness.

For an instant, she debated the merits of making him wait, then decided against it. Given their differing personalities, they'd clash soon enough without any effort on her part. There was no sense in starting off on a sour note. Besides, Gail had set dinner for six-thirty, which meant she'd timed her meal to be ready minutes later. If Christy flexed her proverbial muscles to teach Linc a lesson, she'd also make four people unhappy.

In a way, though, having him fetch her for dinner had that date-night feel to it. Although, she was quick to remind herself, just because it seemed like one on the surface—especially to anyone watching—it didn't mean it was *real*.

Wryly, she glanced down at her own chest, well aware of how deceiving appearances could be.

Linc strode up the walk to Christy's apartment, wondering if the evening would be as full of surprises as the day had been. He'd gone to the hospital as he did every morning, but today he'd been swept into the fundraising tide before he'd realized it. He couldn't say what had prompted him to force Christy into being his dance partner, but if she was going to drag him into her little schemes then it only seemed fair for her to pay the piper, too.

Of course, being her partner didn't pose any great hardship. She was sociable, attractive, and his thoughts toward her weren't always professional. He might even have allowed his sister-in-law to matchmake if Christy didn't have what he considered were several key flaws.

The woman was always haring off on some adventure or getting involved in every cause that came down the pike. While he'd been known to participate in a few adventures himself and had gotten involved in a cause or two of his own, he practiced restraint. Christy, on the other hand, seemed happiest when she flitted from one activity to another. She was like a rolling stone, intent on moving fast and often so she wouldn't gather moss.

His parents, especially his mother, had been like that. He, being the eldest, had always been left to pick up the pieces and he'd vowed he'd never put his children in a similar position.

No, Christy wasn't the one for him, even if she'd captivated him with her looks and her charm. He simply needed a way to get her out of his system and the *Dancing with the Docs* idea seemed tailor-made to do just that. They'd spend time practicing and he'd learn just how unsuitable they were together. Then, and only then, he could forget about her and begin looking for the steady, dependable, down-to-earth woman he really wanted.

Your ideal woman sounds boring, his little voice dared to say.

Maybe so, he admitted, but there was nothing wrong with "boring". Perhaps if his parents had relegated their dream of becoming a superstar country music duo to the past where it had belonged, they wouldn't have driven that lonely stretch of highway halfway between here and

Nashville at four a.m. They'd have been safe in bed, living long enough to see their children grow to adulthood.

As for tonight, he hadn't been able to coax the reason for their gathering from his sister-in-law or his brother, but it had to be important. After the last dinner-party fiasco between the four of them, only a compelling reason would have convinced Gail to repeat the experience.

Gail had been immensely disappointed that he and Christy hadn't clicked together like two cogs, but, as he'd later told her, Christy was everything he wasn't looking for in a romantic partnership. After all the upheavals in his life—his parents' deaths, school, work, college studies, raising siblings—he wanted someone who wasn't in search of the next spine-tingling, hair-raising adventure; someone stable, calm, and content. While it wasn't a bad thing that Christy's friendliness and sunny disposition attracted people like sugar called to ants, he wasn't interested in being one of a crowd of admirers.

Tonight he'd sit through dinner, learn what scheme Gail was up to now, spend the rest of the evening in Ty's den watching whatever sports event was currently televised, then drive Christy home. Dinner with Ty's family wasn't a red-letter occasion, but hanging with them was better than spending time alone.

He leaned on Christy's doorbell, but before the melodic chime barely began, he heard a deep-throated woof followed by thundering paws. Gail had never mentioned her friend owned a dog, so it was entirely possible he'd come to the wrong apartment.

His sister-in-law had told him apartment 4619, but given that the nine was missing from the house number above the porch light, he may have made an error in guessing his prize lay behind this particular door. However, the whimsical fairy stake poked into the pot of impatiens seemed to be the sort of yard ornament Christy would own.

As the footsteps—both human and canine— grew louder, he was already framing an apology for the intrusion when Christy flung open the door with one hand tucked under the black rhinestone-studded collar of a beautiful cream-colored Labrador.

He'd definitely come to the right place.

"Hi," he said inanely, aware he was out of practice when it came to picking up a date.

"Hi, yourself." Christy tugged the dog out of the way. "Come in, please."

He stepped inside and wasn't quite sure if he should look at her or the dog. He wasn't worried about Christy biting a hole in his thigh, though, so he focused on the animal and held out his hand for sniffing purposes. "Who is this lovely lady?"

"Her name is Ria," she said. "She's very protective of me, but she's really a sweetheart."

As expected, Ria sniffed his hand, then licked it, making Linc feel as if he'd passed doggy muster. "I can see that," he said.

She eyed her pet as Ria nudged Linc with her nose. "It appears you two are friends already."

"Dogs usually like me," he said. "Why, I'm not sure." His fondest memories involved pets, but after their family's golden retriever had died of old age when Linc had been sixteen, they'd never replaced him. As it had turned out, a few years later, his hands had been full trying to raising his younger siblings and attend college, without adding the responsibility of a canine.

"Animals are a far better judge of character than we are," she said. "However, Ria doesn't usually give her seal of approval so soon after meeting someone."

"Then I'm flattered." Then, because time was marching on, he asked, "Shall we go?"

Pink suddenly tinged her face. "I'm sorry, but I need a few more minutes."

He couldn't imagine why. She wore a red and white polka-dotted sundress with a matching short-sleeved jacket. Her bare legs were long and tanned and her toenails were painted a matching shade of red and one little toe had a silver ring encircling it.

Wisps of her short reddish-blonde hair framed her face most attractively and seemed to highlight her fine bone structure. From the freckles dancing across the bridge of her nose, she either didn't need makeup to create that warm glow or she only wore just enough to enhance her natural skin tone. He also caught a delightful whiff of citrus and spice that tempted him to lean into her neck and inhale deeply.

Certain she sensed his intense, and appreciative perusal, he met her gaze, hardly able to believe the non-hospital version of the dark-eyed Christy Michaels was so...gorgeous. As far as he was concerned, a few more minutes couldn't improve on the vision in front of him. The idea that he would spend his evening seated across from such delightful eye candy instead of poking inside someone's abdomen suddenly made him anticipate the hours ahead.

"You look great to me," he commented.

Apparently hearing the appreciation in his voice, she smiled. "Thanks, but Ria has carried off my sandals. She does that when she doesn't want me to leave, and now I'm trying to locate where she's stashed them. Would you mind checking around the living room while I go through my bedroom again?"

Ever practical and conscious of the time, he suggested, "You could wear a different pair."

"No can do," she said, plainly impervious to his suggestion. "They match this dress perfectly and nothing else I own will look quite right."

He wanted to argue that it was just the four of them and no one would notice much less care if her sandals coordinated with her dress, but she'd already disappeared down the hallway, leaving him to obey.

"Okay, Ria," he said to the Lab, "where's your favorite hiding place?"

Ria stared at him with a dopey grin on her face.

"No help from you, I see." Linc raised his voice. "Where does she normally hide her treasures?"

"Under the furniture," she called back, "or in her toy box."

Linc glanced around the great room and decided that Christy lived a relatively spartan existence. She didn't own a lot of furniture and other than a few silk flower arrangements scattered around, the surfaces were free of what he called dust-collectors, although none would pass the white-glove treatment.

Spartan or not, however, the room had that cluttered, lived-in feel. Decorative pillows were thrown haphazardly, a fuzzy Southwestern print afghan was tossed carelessly over one armchair, and women's magazines were gathered in untidy heaps on the floor.

Dutifully, he peeked under the floral-print sofa and found a few mismatched but brightly colored socks. Some were knee-length and others were just footies, but each one sported varying sizes of chew holes. Next, he moved to the matching side chair where he unearthed two pairs of silk panties—one black and one fire-engine-red—that couldn't claim more than a dollar's worth of fabric between them.

After adding the lingerie to his pile, he pinched the bridge of his nose and told himself to forget what he'd just seen and touched. Knowing her tastes ran along those kinds of lines, when he saw her on duty again, he'd have a difficult time keeping his mind off what might be underneath her scrub suit.

Shoot, why wait until then? His imagination was already running wild over what color underwear she was wearing under her sundress.

He carefully glanced around the room in search of something resembling a doggie toy box and found a wicker basket tucked on the bottom shelf of the bookcase in the corner filled with playthings that a canine would love. Resting on his haunches, he rummaged through a pile of half-chewed dog bones, several balls and Frisbees, a short rope, and an assortment of stuffed animals before he struck bottom.

"No shoes in here," he called out as he rose.

"Thanks for checking," she answered back.

His watch chimed the quarter-hour. "We really should be going."

"Just a few more minutes. I promise."

Because he had so little time for leisure reading, the books on her shelves drew his gaze next, and he took a few minutes to glance at the titles. Most of her paperbacks were romances with a few adventure novels sprinkled among them. He also ran across several cookbooks and a few exercise DVDs, but tucked among them were a few books that piqued his curiosity.

Chicken Soup for the Survivor's Soul. Life after Cancer. Foods that Fight. Staying Fit after Chemo.

Before he could wonder what had caused her interest in such topics, she returned to the living room, wearing a pair of strappy red high-heeled sandals that emphasized her shapely legs. "Sorry about the wait," she said breathlessly. "I found them in my laundry basket."

"Great. By the way, I ran across a few things you might have lost." He plucked his pile of treasures off the coffee table and handed them to her.

Her face turned a lovely shade of pink as she eyed the scraps on top. "I wondered where those had gone," she said, her chuckle quite pleasing to his ears. "I've blamed the washing machine all this time. Ria, you've been a bad girl."

Ria sank onto her belly and placed her head on her front paws.

"But I love you anyway," she said as she crouched down to scratch behind the dog's ears. "Now, behave while we're gone."

As she rubbed, Ria responded with a contented sigh and a blissful doggy smile before rolling over onto her back for a tummy rub. Obviously Christy had The Touch, and immediately he wanted to feel her fingers working their magic on *his* sore spots.

He tore his gaze from the sight, reminding himself that Christy wasn't his type even if she could engender all sorts of unrealistic thoughts. She was too perky, too lively, and too *everything*. Women like her weren't content with the mundane aspects of living. They wanted the constant stimulation of social activities, four-star shopping and exotic vacations. Staying home for popcorn and a movie would be considered slumming.

"Are we ready now?" he asked, conscious of his peevish tone when all he wanted to do was shake these wicked mental pictures out of his head.

She straightened. "Of course. Sorry to keep you waiting."

To his regret, the warm note in her voice had disappeared and he wondered what it would take to bring it back. If he walked into his brother's house with icicles hanging in the air, his sister-in-law would read him the Riot Act. He didn't know why Gail was so protective of Christy, but she was.

Minutes later, Linc found himself on the sidewalk, accompanying her to his car. He couldn't explain why he found the need to rest his hand on the small of her back—it wasn't as if the sidewalk was icy and he intended to keep her from falling—but he did.

That small, politely ingrained action made him wonder if his plan to concentrate on his career should be revised. He was thirty-seven now and he had to admit that at times he grew weary of his own company. To make matters worse, lately, being around Gail and Ty made him realize just how much he was missing.

Now was one of those moments. Especially when he caught a glimpse of a well-formed knee and a trim ankle as he helped her into the passenger seat.

He might be physically attracted to Christy Michaels, but their temperaments made them polar opposites. He had enough drama in his life and when he came home at night, he wanted someone to share his quiet and peaceable existence, not someone who thrived on being the life of a party.

Opposites or not, though, he wasn't going to pass the drive in chilly silence. Given how much she obviously loved Ria, he knew exactly how to break the ice.

"After seeing your dog, I'm wondering if I should get one," he commented as he slid behind the wheel.

"They're a lot of work, but the companionship is worth every minute," she said. "Did you have a breed in mind?"

"No, but I'd lean toward a collie or a retriever. We had one when I was a kid. Skipper died of old age, but we didn't replace him."

She nodded. "I can understand that. Bringing a new pet home can make you feel guilty—like you're replacing them as easily as you replace a worn-out pair of socks—when in actuality, you aren't replacing them because they'll always be a part of you, no matter what."

Spoken like a true dog lover, he thought, impressed by her insight.

"Why don't you have a dog now?" she asked.

"Isn't it obvious? A pet doesn't fit into my lifestyle."

"Oh." He heard a wealth of emotion—mainly disappointment—in the way she uttered that one word. It was almost as if she found him lacking when she should have been impressed by his thoughtfulness. After all, the poor mutt would be the one suffering from inattention.

"You're probably right," she added politely. "They do have a habit of ruining the best-laid plans."

The conversation flagged, and he hated that the relaxed mood between them had become strained once again. Wasn't there anything they could discuss without venturing into rocky territory? If he didn't do something to lighten the tension, they'd face an uncomfortable evening ahead of them. He'd already promised Gail he'd be on his best behavior, so he had to repair the damage before they arrived.

Recalling another subject in which she'd seemed quite passionate, he asked, "Any word on the festival fundraiser idea?"

"According to Denise, it's a go." To his relief, the lilt in her voice had returned, although her revelation wasn't the news he'd wanted to hear.

"I was afraid of that."

"Still worried about dancing in front of people?"

"Not worried," he corrected. "Uncomfortable."

"As a surgeon, you should be used to being in the spotlight."

"Yes, but it isn't the same spotlight," he insisted. In the OR, he actually knew what he was doing and was at ease in his own skin. Sailing around a dance floor didn't compare.

"The problem is, my schedule for the next month is a killer and lessons are out of the question," he explained. "My partners are going on vacation and—"

"No one said you had to take lessons," she pointed out.

The motto he'd lived by was simple. *Anything worth doing was worth doing well.* If he was going to participate in this dancing thing, then he'd put forth his best effort.

"Whatever we do at the time of the competition will be fine with me," she added. "If you just want to stand and sway to the music, I'll be happy."

"You told me this morning it wouldn't be good enough," he accused.

She shrugged. "I changed my mind. I'm not participating to win a prize."

He didn't think the possibility of taking first place was her motive. She was simply one of those people who threw herself into whatever project caught her fancy, which was also why he disagreed with her remark about being happy. Christy had too much vim and vigor to be content with a lackluster performance. Even *he* wasn't satisfied and he was far less outgoing than she was.

All of which meant that he was going to have to carve out time in his schedule for lessons—lessons that involved holding this woman with her citrusy scent and skimpy underwear in his arms.

Merely picturing those moments was enough to send his blood tumbling through his body at a fast and furious rate. The things a man had to do for charity...

Christy had known her evening was off to a bad start when Ria hid her shoes. She'd hoped to find them before Linc arrived but, as luck would have it, she hadn't. Although he'd been polite about it, clearly the delay had taxed his patience and his perfectly timed schedule.

Yet she'd enjoyed the little courtesies he'd shown her. Being in the close confines of his vehicle, she'd been painfully aware of his fresh, clean scent to the point her throat went dry.

Of all the men in her circle of friends and acquaintances, why did *he* have to be the one who oozed sex appeal? After feeling his hand at her waist, she honestly didn't know how she'd survive an evening as his dance partner.

To make matters worse, Gail had seated her next to him at the dinner table and his arm had brushed against hers on several occasions as they'd passed the food.

Maybe she needed to call an escort service in order to calm those suddenly raging hormones, but her fear of rejection was too strong to risk it. If a man who'd supposedly loved her hadn't been able to handle her diagnosis and resultant treatment, who else could?

No, better that she hurry home after dinner, take Ria for a long run at the dog park until they were both too tired to do more than curl up on the sofa with a carton of frozen chocolate yogurt, a handful of dog treats, and a sappy movie on the TV screen.

Linc's voice forced her to focus on her surroundings. "Okay, you two. What's up? And don't tell me 'Nothing' because I know you both too well to believe otherwise."

Gail and Ty looked at each other with such an expression of love between them that Christy was half-jealous. Made a little uncomfortable by their silent exchange, she glanced at Linc and immediately noticed the similarities between the brothers.

They had the same bone structure, the same complexion, and the same shade of brown hair. Both Maguire males were handsome but, to her, Linc's features were far more interesting—probably because life had left its imprint on them. According to Gail, as the oldest brother, Linc had stepped into his parents' role after their deaths in a car accident when he was nineteen and he'd guided his younger siblings through their rocky teenage years. It was only logical that the sudden responsibility had formed him into the driven, purposeful man he was today.

Christy glanced at her dark-haired friend and saw the gentle smile on her face. "You're pregnant again?" she guessed.

Gail patted her husband's hand as she shook her head. "No. But maybe we can announce that when we get back."

"Get back? Where are you going?"

Ty answered his brother's question. "Paris."

Christy was stunned…and envious. It was one of the cities she'd put on the bucket list she'd created during her chemotherapy sessions. "Oh, how fun. I've always wanted to go there."

Linc didn't seem to share her excitement. "Paris? As in France? Or Paris, as in Texas?"

"France," Ty told him. "My company is opening an overseas branch and they want a computer consultant to be on site. They chose me."

Linc reached across the table to shake his brother's hand. "Congratulations. You've worked hard for this. I'm proud of you. How long will you be gone?"

Ty exchanged a glance with Gail. "Two months, give or take a few weeks, depending on how well the project progresses. Because Gail knows the secretarial ropes of our firm, my boss has offered to send her as my assistant."

Theirs had been an office romance and after Derek had arrived, Gail had cut her work status to part time.

"And the kids?" Christy thought of six-year-old Emma and eight-year-old Derek, who'd already been excused from the table to play outside with their friends. "What about them?"

Gail's expression turned hopeful. "That's why you're both here tonight. We wanted to ask a favor."

"Anything," she promptly replied.

"Would you and Linc be their guardians and take care of them while we're gone?"

CHAPTER TWO

CHRISTY was overwhelmed by their request but in her mind she didn't have any doubts as to her answer. She loved the Maguire children and she couldn't wait to step into a temporary mom role. Because of her diagnosis and the resultant treatment, she'd already resigned herself to the possibility that Ria might be the closest thing to ever having a child of her own, so the idea of acting as a fill-in mother was exciting.

She was also quite aware that Gail had chosen *her* out of all their friends and family to take on this responsibility. Okay, so they'd asked Linc, too, but he didn't really count. His work was his life and by his own admission his schedule for the next few weeks was packed. For all intents and purposes, she'd be on her own.

It was a heady thought.

It was also quite daunting.

She started to speak, but Gail forestalled her.

"Christy, I know you'll immediately agree because it's in your nature to help out a friend. And, Linc, I know you'll accept because you're family, but before either of you commit yourselves, I want you to know *exactly* what you'd be letting yourselves in for. And if either of you have second thoughts, we won't be hurt or upset."

"Okay," Christy said, certain she wouldn't change her mind no matter what Gail and Ty told them. "We're listening."

"First, we'd expect you to live here because it will be best if Derek and Emma stick with the familiar."

Christy hadn't considered that, but Gail's plan made perfect sense. Living in their home wouldn't pose any hardship whatsoever. What it would require, though, was coordination between her schedule and Linc's to be sure they covered every hour of every day, and she was curious how Gail had ironed that small but important detail. No doubt, she'd learn the answer shortly.

"What about Ria?" she asked. "I'd hate to board her for that length of time."

"She's welcome, too," Ty answered. "In fact, I know the kids would be thrilled. They've been asking for a dog for some time, and looking after

Ria will give them a taste of what pet ownership is about."

Satisfied by how easily that potential problem had been averted, Christy relaxed. She imagined her Labrador and the kids playing Frisbee in the large Maguire back yard and could hear the children's laughter interspersed with Ria's excited woofs. They'd have a great time.

"Second," Gail continued, "the fall term starts next week so the kids will already be in a routine before we leave the week after that. On the days Christy doesn't work, you'll have to take them to school and pick them up at four, which shouldn't pose a problem.

"The days you both work are little trickier as there's a two-hour window when Linc would be on his own. One of the neighborhood high-school girls—Heather—can come by around six-thirty to fix breakfast and take them to school. She'll come sooner to cover that window if Linc's on call, but you'll have to let her know the night before.

"Then, at the end of the day, the kids can walk across the street to the church's after-school day-care until Christy's shift ends at five. The day-

care is open until seven, so that works out well."
She smiled. "Repeat as necessary."

"It sounds as if you've thought of everything,"
Christy said.

"We tried," Gail answered.

"Do Emma and Derek know you're asking me?"
As Linc stiffened beside her, she corrected herself. "I mean *us*?"

"It was the only way they'd agree to being left
behind," Gail admitted ruefully. "I suspect they
think you'll cater to their every whim. I know
what a pushover you are, Christy..." she softened
her statement with a smile "...so I'm counting on
you to be firm."

"Be firm," she repeated. "Got it."

"Don't kid yourself," Ty warned. "They'll push
you to the max. You can't be the benevolent aunt
and uncle. This isn't a weekend vacation."

"In other words, you expect us to give them a
healthy breakfast, send them to bed on time, and
eat dinner before dessert," Linc said.

His sidelong glance made Christy wonder if
he'd mentioned those things purely for her benefit. Didn't he think she had an ounce of common sense? He obviously suspected she'd offer
cookies and cake for breakfast, lunch, and din-

ner, and let them stay up as late as they pleased.
While she didn't consider herself a rule-breaker,
she also knew that every moment should be lived
to its fullest. If a few rules had to be broken on
occasion, then so be it.

Now that she'd raised the question in her mind,
she took it a step further. Did he have the same
lack of faith in her nursing skills as he obviously
did in her parenting abilities? There hadn't been
a single incident when he'd questioned her patient
care, but she'd ask him when they were alone.

"We're asking a lot from both of you," Ty added,
"but you were first on our list."

"I appreciate the vote of confidence," Christy
said. "Count me in."

"Me, too," Linc added. "We only need to choose
which days are yours and which are mine."

She nodded, although she would have preferred
having Linc suggest that she be their sole care-
taker while he filled in when his schedule allowed. Clearly, he wanted equal, or as near equal,
time as possible.

Darn the man!

"Actually, we want you both to stay here," Gail
said. "Together."

Christy met Linc's startled gaze and guessed

that her own surprise mirrored his. "At the same time?" she asked redundantly.

Gail nodded. "That way, if Linc gets called out for a patient in the middle of the night, he won't have to worry about the kids because you're just down the hall. You two won't have to rearrange and juggle your own schedules, so it'll be less disruptive for everyone."

They wanted her to stay here, in their house, with Linc? Christy had a difficult time wrapping her brain around that concept. While they were amicable enough to each other at the hospital, being together twenty-four seven meant they'd drive each other crazy within a week, and then where would the kids be? Most likely in the middle of a war zone.

What concerned her even more, though, was the simple question of how would she handle being in such close proximity to a guy she found so attractive? If seeing him in a scrub suit and interacting with him on a purely professional basis made her nervous and sent her imagination soaring, how would she manage if she saw that handsome smile, those broad shoulders on a regular, casual basis?

"This is how we want it," Gail said, as if she

sensed Christy's reservations. "The kids will handle our absence better if they stay in their normal surroundings. That's not to say they can't spend a night or two elsewhere, but we'd feel better knowing they're in familiar territory and in the same homey, two-parent environment."

"We know it won't be easy for either of you because you're both so fiercely independent, so if it's a problem, we can ask someone else," Ty said.

Miss the opportunity to pamper Gail's kids? Not a chance. Yes, Linc would probably drive her crazy with his rigid, no-time-to-stop-and-smell-the-roses attitude, but she was an adult. She could handle the inevitable clashes.

On the other hand, Linc went to work early and stayed late. Chances were they wouldn't see each other until the kids went to bed. Afterward, they could each slink into their separate corners.

It was a workable plan, she decided. If it wasn't, she'd dream up a Plan B. Emma and Derek's well-being was what mattered, not her personal preferences.

"If you can handle the arrangements we've outlined—"

"Piece of cake," Christy said, although the idea

of living under the same roof as Linc gave her some pause.

"Not a problem," Linc added. "We can learn to live with each other for a few weeks."

"Good. Then it's settled." Gail beamed. "You don't know what a relief this is for us."

As Christy glanced around the table, Gail was the only one who seemed remotely satisfied with the arrangement. She saw a combination of speculation and caution in Ty's eyes as he studied his brother. Linc's squared jaw and the chiseled lines around his mouth reflected resignation rather than enthusiasm. No doubt her reservations were clear on her face as well.

Living under the same roof was only a two-month gig or less, she consoled herself, and those six or eight weeks were nothing more than a single pebble along life's riverbed. She could endure *anything* for that length of time, because the benefits of being with Emma and Derek overshadowed the potential problems. If she could survive breast cancer, she could handle Lincoln Maguire's idiosyncrasies.

"I know what you're going to say." Ty held up his hands to forestall Linc's comments the moment the two of them were alone on the shaded back-yard patio, "but before you unload, hear me out."

Linc took a swig from his bottle of cold root beer. "I'm listening."

"You're upset we asked Christy to help you, but honestly our decision is no reflection on your parenting abilities. You've had the kids before and they came back raving about the great time they had. They love you and I know you love them."

He did. No matter how busy he was, he'd move heaven and earth for his niece and nephew. They were his family, and even if he wasn't in any hurry to have one of his own, those bonds were still important to him.

"I can't imagine a single scenario you can't handle by yourself with your eyes closed and one hand tied behind your back," Ty added loyally.

"Thanks for the vote of confidence."

"After all," Ty continued, "you kept us on the straight and narrow when you were hardly out of your teenage years yourself. Joanie and I weren't angels either, if I recall. I'm sure there were times when you wanted to tear out your hair, and ours, too, but you didn't. When you finally decide to focus on your personal life instead of your professional one, you're going to be a great dad."

Linc recognized Ty's strategy. "You can stop heaping on the praise, pip-squeak," he affectionately told his brother. "In the middle of all that, I know there's a 'but'."

Ty grinned sheepishly. "I never could fool you for long, could I? The thing is, we're talking two months. You don't have the usual nine-to-five job, and we had to think of a contingency plan for the times you work late, go in early, or get called out in the wee hours, because we don't expect you to put your doctor business on hold for us."

Linc shifted in his chair, suddenly uncomfortable at hearing how lonely his life sounded, even if the description was uncannily accurate.

"I'll confess that sharing the responsibility with another person bothered me," he admitted soberly, "but your way is best for the kids' well-being. I even see your point about asking us to stay here *together*."

He saw the logic behind their request, but he didn't like it, especially now that he'd seen those small scraps of silk Christy called underwear. How was he supposed to focus on the youngsters when a picture of her wearing a pair of those and just a smile kept popping into his head at the most inopportune times?

He might not find fault with her nursing skills, but taking care of patients wasn't the same as maintaining a home and looking after the needs of two children on a round-the-clock basis.

Did she even know how to boil water? If the stories circulating about her were to be believed—and he didn't dispute them because he'd heard her share some of them herself—she rarely sat still long enough for such mundane things. Canoeing down the Amazon, skydiving in California, white-water rafting in Colorado, cross-country motor-cycle trips and a few laps around the Daytona 500 speedway were only part of her repertoire of experiences.

Lessons from Martha Stewart or Rachel Ray weren't on the list.

Her culinary skills aside, he hoped she had more redeeming qualities than being Gail's friend who was the life of every party and who owned a dog that Emma and Derek loved. As far as he was concerned, they could have handled the nights he was on call on a case-by-case basis, but if this was how his brother wanted it, then he would suf-fer in silence.

"I'm glad you're being a good sport about this," Ty said. "And when you feel your control slipping over the edge, think of your circumstances as some of the medicine you forced down our throats as kids." He grinned. "It tastes terrible going down, but in the end it cures what ails you."

Two weeks later, Christy made a point to hang around the nurses' station to lie in wait for Linc. Ever since their dinner with Gail and Ty, he'd slipped in and out of their unit like a wraith. She knew he was extra-busy right now, with one of his partners on vacation, but she wasn't completely convinced that he wasn't avoiding her as well.

As of tonight they'd more or less be living together and she had a few issues she wanted to iron out before they actually became roomies, but those would have to wait. Her patient, Jose Lopez, a recent ruptured appendix case, concerned her.

Her patience paid off. Linc strode in shortly before eight looking more handsome than a man who had spent his day with sick people had a right to. His yellow polo shirt stretched across his shoulders and his hair had a damp curl as if he'd just got out of the shower.

He didn't walk with a cocky swagger but carried himself with a quiet confidence that suggested no problem was too big for him to solve. She certainly hoped so because today she had one.

She immediately cornered him before he could disappear into a patient room.

"I don't like the way Jose, Mr Lopez, looks," she said without preamble.

"Okay," he said with equanimity. "What's his complaint?"

"He doesn't have one, as such."

He lifted one eyebrow. "You aren't giving me much to go on. A diagnosis of 'He doesn't look right' isn't strong enough to justify a battery of tests."

Her face warmed under his rebuke. Other physicians would have attributed her impression as that proverbial gut feeling no one could afford to ignore, but clearly Lincoln Maguire didn't believe in intuition. He only wanted cold, hard evidence. As far as she was concerned, he'd answered her private question about what he thought of her nursing savvy.

"I realize that," she said stiffly, her spine straight, "which is why I've been watching him. He doesn't complain about pain as such, but he finally admitted he has a few twinges because I've caught him rubbing his chest. According to the nursing notes, he received an antacid for heart-burn several times during the night."

"You don't think heartburn is a possibility?" he asked.

"No," she said bluntly, "but only because I think his skin color is off."

He retrieved the chart on the computer and began perusing the notes. "How are his oxygen sats?"

"On the low end of normal."

"Shortness of breath?"

She shook her head. "He said his chest some-times feels a little tight, but that's all."

He stared thoughtfully at the computer before meeting her gaze. "It could be anything and it could be nothing."

"I know, which is why I wanted to ask you to check him thoroughly."

He hesitated for a fraction of a second before he shrugged. "Okay. Duly noted. I'll see what I can find."

She'd been half-afraid he'd dismiss her con-cerns, so she was grateful to hear of his inten-tions to follow through. And because she was relieved to pass the burden onto his shoulders, she chose to make small talk as they strode toward the room. "Are you ready for tonight?"

"I am," he said. "Do you need help taking anything over to Ty's house?"

"Not now," she said. "I'm only moving some clothes and a few books. What I don't bring now, I can always get later."

"Fair enough." He strode into Lopez's room and the subject was closed.

Christy watched and listened as Linc checked his patient, seeming much more congenial with Jose than with her, but, then, a lot of the nurses had said he was far more personable with his patients than with the staff. She took some comfort in that because she'd begun to wonder if he was only uncomfortable around her.

"I hear you're having a few chest twinges," Linc mentioned as he pulled out his stethoscope and listened to Jose's heart and lung sounds.

"Some. It's happening more often than it did yesterday, though. Sometimes I cough for no reason," the forty-year-old replied. Jose was of average height, but between his wife's reportedly fantastic cooking and his years as a stonemason, he was built like the bricks he laid for a living. "Do you think it's the hospital food? Maybe it's giving me the heartburn." His tanned, leathery face broke into a smile.

Linc laughed. "If you're hinting that you want me to give Francesca permission to bring you some of her famous enchiladas, you'll be disappointed."

"It was worth a try, Doc."

Christy watched the friendly exchange, stunned by how Linc's smile made him seem so… *normal.* Clearly, the man did have moments when he wasn't completely focused on his work, but she'd gone on countless rounds with him over the past year and had never heard such a heartfelt sound. She would have remembered if she had. Somehow, she sensed the two of them had more than a simple doctor-patient relationship, which only made her curious as to what connection a blue-collar worker like Jose had with the highly successful general surgeon.

He flung the stethoscope around his neck. "A few more days and you can eat her cooking to your heart's content. Meanwhile, though, I want to check out these little twinges and the cough you're having. We're going to run a few tests so be prepared for everything from X-rays and EKGs to blood work."

Jose's expression sobered. "You think it's my heart?"

"Not necessarily. If your chest feels tight and you're noticing a cough, pneumonia is a concern," he said, "so I'm going to try and discover what's going on. As you said, you may only have heartburn but, to be thorough, we're going to check out everything. Okay?"

His confidence was reassuring because Jose's face relaxed. It was obvious why Linc's patients loved him, and why he was so very busy.

"Are you having any pain in your legs?" Linc asked.

Jose wrinkled his face in thought. "I had a charley horse earlier in my right calf, but it's gone now."

Linc immediately flung back the sheet and checked his legs. "We'll look into that, too," he said, sounding unconcerned, "and as soon as I get those results, we'll let you know what we've found. Okay?" He patted Jose's shoulder before he left.

Outside Lopez's room, Christy immediately pounced. "Then I was right. You found something."

"Not really," he admitted.

"Oh." Her good spirits deflated.

"Are you sure his condition has changed in the last twenty-four hours?"

She knew what her intuition was telling her and she wasn't going to back down. "He said himself he has a cough and his chest feels tight," she reminded him. "Now he has a muscle spasm in his leg. Those are new symptoms."

He looked thoughtful for a moment. "Okay," he said decisively. "I want a chest X-ray, a Doppler exam on his legs, and blood drawn for a blood count, a cardiac panel and a D-dimer test."

She recognized the latter as one used to diagnose the presence of a blood clot. "Do you suspect a PE?" She used the shorthand for pulmonary embolism.

"I suspect a lot of things, but in the interest of ruling out as much as we can we'll add that to the list of possibilities. I also want a CT scan of his lungs and if the results are inconclusive, I want a VQ scan."

The CT scan was a quick way to detect a blood clot, but not every clot was detected using this procedure, which meant the next step was the VQ scan. The two-part ventilation-perfusion procedure used both injected and aerosolized radioactive material to show the amount of blood and air flowing through the lungs. Naturally, if the patterns were abnormal, intervention was required.

"I'll get right on it," she said.

"And call me ASAP with those results," he ordered in the brisk tone she knew so well.

As Christy placed the various orders into the computer system, she was hoping the tests would show something to support her nagging intuition, although she hoped it would be something relatively uncomplicated.

Several hours later the results were in. Shortly after Christy phoned him with the radiologist's report, Linc appeared on the unit. Asking for her to join him, he marched directly into his patient's room.

"Jose," he said briskly, "I have news on your tests."

Jose nodded his salt-and-pepper head. "I had a feeling something was wrong when they stuck me in that fancy X-ray machine," he said. "How bad is it?"

"You have a very small blood clot in your leg and a small one in your lung, which isn't good," Linc said bluntly.

"But you can fix it. Right?"

Christy recognized the hope and the uncertainty on the man's face. She knew exactly how he felt.

"This is where I give you the good news," Linc said kindly. "I'm going to start you on a variety of blood thinners and other drugs that will work to dissolve the clots so they don't break off and plug a major vessel. It'll take time—you won't be cured overnight—but eventually you should be fine."

Jose leaned head back against the pillows in obvious relief.

"The other good news is that you had a nurse who was on the ball so we could catch the problem early," Linc said as he eyed Christy. "A lot of patients aren't that fortunate."

"And I should be fine?" Jose repeated, clearly wanting reassurance that the final outcome would be positive.

"Yes."

After a few more minutes of discussing Jose's treatment plan, they left. Outside the room Linc pulled her aside. "Increase his oxygen and keep a close eye on him. I want to know if there's a change, no matter how slight."

"Okay."

"Tomorrow, we'll—" he began.

"It's Saturday," she reminded him. "I'm off duty. Emma and Derek, remember?"

He looked surprised, as if for a minute he'd forgotten what day it was. "Then I'll see you tonight," he said.

"Before or after dinner?"

"Before, I suppose. Why?"

She was flying high on her success, so she couldn't hold back from teasing him. "Just checking to see if I can serve dessert as the appetizer or not."

His eyes narrowed ever so slightly. "You're kidding, aren't you?"

"Of course I am," she responded pertly. "Contrary to what you might think, I can exercise self-control and I do use the gray matter between my ears from time to time."

His eyes suddenly gleamed with humor. "I stand corrected. Either way, though, I'll be at the house in time to take Gail and Ty to the airport."

She received the distinct impression that he would move heaven and earth to do so. It also occurred to her that he might be as reluctant to see his brother leave as his niece and nephew were.

"Okay, we'll save you a piece of cake."

"Do that. By the way, good work with Lopez today."

His unexpected praise only added to her high spirits. "Thanks."

"See you tonight," he said, before he turned on one heel and left.

She stared at his backside until he rounded the corner, startled by how *husbandly* he'd sounded. Suddenly she realized that not only would she see him tonight, she'd see him *every* night thereafter, too.

It also meant that every night he'd drop the trappings of his profession and she wouldn't have the barrier of the doctor-nurse relationship to keep her wicked imagination in check. He'd appear as a normal guy—one who mowed the grass, took out the trash, left dirty dishes in the sink, and woke up every morning with his hair mussed and a whiskery shadow on his face.

Anticipation shivered down her spine.

She was being completely unreasonable.

Linc walked into the kitchen of Gail and Ty's house with his small entourage and fought to keep his voice even-tempered. It had been a long day in his practice and seeing off his younger brother to another country for two months—*Paris*, no less—had been far more emotionally draining than he'd expected. He'd left his twenties behind ages ago and was a highly respected surgeon, yet he felt as lost as he had when he'd moved Ty into his first apartment.

Ty might not need him in that big-brother-knows-best role, but it was still hard to accept whenever the fact hit him between the eyes. No, he wanted to veg out with nothing more mentally or emotionally taxing than a game of checkers with Derek or a tea party with Emma, but if Christy had her way, it wouldn't happen.

"Going out to dinner when Gail has a refrigerator full of food waiting for us is unnecessary," he pointed out. "Need I also remind you it's Friday night?" Which meant every restaurant was packed and would be for quite a while.

"I know it's Friday and I agree that eating out isn't *necessary*," she said with a hint of steel underneath her sweet tone, "but it would be *fun*."

He rubbed his face. *Fun* was going to become a four-letter word if every activity had to be measured against that standard. "We have all weekend for fun."

She rubbed the back of her neck in a frustrated

gesture and drew a deep breath. "I realize that," she finally said, "but look at those two. Don't you think they need something as a pick-me-up *now*, rather than tomorrow?"

He glanced at Derek and noticed his slumped posture in the straight-backed chair, his ball cap pulled low as he rested his chin on his propped arm. Emma sat beside him and occasionally wiped her eyes and sniffled as her thin shoulders shook. Christy's Lab stood between the two, gazing at one then the other, as if trying to decide which one needed her comfort more.

They made a dejected picture, which was only understandable. They'd just driven home from the airport after saying goodbye to their parents and the reality of the situation had hit them hard.

"I agree they're down in the dumps, but a fast-food hamburger won't make them feel better."

"You might be surprised." She clapped her hands. "Hey, kids, how does a picnic sound? Ria needs a spin around the dog park and while she's running around with her buddies, we'll enjoy our dinner in the great outdoors."

A picnic, at seven o'clock at night, with dark clouds rolling in and rain in the forecast, wasn't Linc's idea of fun. While the kids didn't seem overly enthusiastic with her suggestion, interest flickered in Derek's eyes and Emma's shoulders stopped shaking as she gazed expectantly at Christy. Apparently Ria recognized the word *park* because her ears suddenly perked and her tail wagged.

"Then it's settled," she declared, although as far as Linc was concerned she'd simply made an executive decision. Because he knew they had to do something drastic or the entire evening would remain miserable for everyone, he let it stand. "Everyone can make his or her own sandwich and then we're off."

Before Linc could wonder where the dog park actually was, Christy had emptied the refrigerator and created an assembly line of fixings. "Who wants to be first?" she asked.

The two children rushed to her side and began assembling their sandwiches with her help. Linc hovered in the background, ready to kill the idea if the kids gave him the slightest bit of encouragement.

They didn't. In fact, he would never have thought the idea of a picnic would have turned the mood around so quickly. Ordinary sandwiches suddenly became gourmet delights under

Christy's tutelage. Every now and then a tasty nugget would fall and an ever-vigilant Ria would snap up the evidence.

He noticed Derek had made himself a man-sized meal while Emma's dinner was a dainty mix of meat, cheese, and pickles sliced into four perfect triangles. Christy, he'd noticed, used a special roll and included lots of lettuce and tomato as well as thinly sliced cucumbers, avocado, and black olives on a thin layer of slivered turkey.

She glanced at him with a raised eyebrow. "You'd better start assembling or you'll end up without."

"Yours looks so good, maybe you can make an extra," he said hopefully.

"Sorry. Dinner tonight is self-service." She slid the package of rolls in his direction. "He who doesn't fix his own doesn't eat."

"Yeah, Unca Linc," Emma said as she speared olives onto her fingers and began eating them. "You have to get in the spirit. Ria and I are gonna play catch with her Frisbee. Wanna play with us?"

"We'll see," he said as he opened a roll and piled on his ingredients. Just before he was ready to position the top part of the bun, Christy held up a shaker.

"What's that?" he asked.

"A little extra flavor," she said. "Garlic, onion, and few other spices. Want to try some?"

Three people's gazes rested on him and each one reflected open curiosity, as if they were expecting him to refuse. Was he that predictable?

"Sure, why not?" he said. "Tonight's a night to throw caution to the wind and have fun. Who cares about bad breath? Right, kids?"

"Right," they echoed.

Yet as he watched Christy pop a slice of avocado into her kissable mouth, he realized there was an advantage to having garlic breath. He wouldn't be tempted to do something immensely stupid on their first night together.

Soon they were on their way with food and bottled drinks in the ice chest, a few blankets, Ria's toys and water bowl. By the time they'd arrived at the dog park, Christy had led them in a noisy rendition of "B-I-N-G-O" that made his ears hurt.

"Aren't you going to sing?" Christy asked him when the group stopped momentarily for breath.

He couldn't stop a smile, neither did he want to because the excitement had become infectious. "First you roped me into dancing, and now you expect me to become a vocalist? A man has to draw the line somewhere," he said, pretending affront.

"Spoilsport." She obviously didn't take offense because she chuckled, then immediately led them in the next stanza.

As he looked into the back seat in the rearview mirror, hearing Emma and Derek's laughter was far better than seeing them with sad faces, so he didn't have the heart to tell them to tone down the noise level.

He also didn't have the heart to scold them for eating only half of their food because they were in such a rush to play with Ria before the rain fell.

"They're going to be starving later," he said as Christy wrapped up their sandwiches.

"Probably," she agreed, "but their sandwiches will keep. How's your dinner?"

He polished off his last bite before grabbing a bunch of red grapes. "Delicious."

"Then we should do this more often."

"Maybe," he said, unwilling to commit.

"Food always tastes better eaten outside."

He glanced around the park, noting that several other families had taken advantage of the picnic tables. "Oh, I don't know," he mused, thinking of ants and flies and a host of other associated nuisances, not to mention spilled drinks and sticky hands. "It isn't always a great experience."

She chuckled. "Let me guess. Your idea of eating outside is gobbling down a bagel or a burger while you're stuck in traffic."

It was uncanny how accurately she could read him and they'd hardly spent any time together. How much of his soul would she see by the end of two months? "Yeah," he admitted.

"That doesn't count. You have to soak up the ambience of your surroundings. Allow nature's scents of pine and honeysuckle and lavender to mingle with the aroma of the food." She inhaled. "That's what dining outdoors is all about."

As she closed her eyes, he had the strangest urge to trace the line of her jaw with his fingertips and kiss away the fleck of avocado on the corner of her mouth. He also wanted to see if her strawberry-blonde hair was as soft as it looked, discover if she'd fit against his body as perfectly as he imagined.

Giving in to temptation wasn't a wise thing to do. He simply had to deny that sudden attraction because if he didn't, it would only create more problems in the long run. They were only two people who shared the responsibility of two kids for a few weeks. Nothing more, nothing less.

And yet her soft skin beckoned and his fingers itched to explore...

A sudden crack of thunder told him the storm would arrive soon. Immediately, he rose. "Come on, kids. Time to load up and head for home."

As the children scampered back to their picnic table, with Ria keeping pace, he was once again grateful to see smiles on their faces.

"They really needed this, didn't they?" he mused as he helped Christy pack up the ice chest.

"Of course they did. Otherwise they would have moped all evening."

"Bedtime still could be rocky," he warned.

"Probably," she admitted, "but why do you think I wanted them to chase Ria? I predict they'll be too tired to think much about their parents being gone."

"And if they do?"

"Then we give them something to look forward to tomorrow. Before they know it, one day will slide into another and the weeks will fly by."

She was right. His whole life had been about staying busy and the years had blended together. Other than a few milestones to mark the passage of time, including his birthday, one month wasn't any different than the next.

"I hope you're right. In any case, your picnic idea was brilliant."

She laughed. "Oh, my. Two compliments in one day. You aren't feverish, are you?"

As she placed her palm on his forehead, his heart immediately pounded to a double-time beat. He was hot all right, but it had nothing to do a virus and everything to do with her.

CHAPTER THREE

"TELL me the story of the princess again, Unca Linc," Emma demanded.

"We read Penelope's tale already," he told her.

"Not hers. I want to hear the one you have in your head."

Christy smiled at the sight of the six-year-old, wearing her frilly pink nightgown, snuggled under Linc's left arm, while Derek, clad in camouflage pj's, lounged on the chair's opposite arm.

What struck her most with the scene was how comfortable Linc appeared. His smiles were wide and his touch gentle as he tousled Derek's damp hair and tickled Emma's ear.

How had she ever thought him cold and unfeeling?

"Aw, Emma, not again," Derek moaned. "I want to hear the knight story and how he killed the dragon and slept under the stars with his trusty steed, Thunder."

"Trusty steed?" Christy chimed in as she perched on the edge of the sofa. "Oh, I want to hear about him, too."

Linc cast an exasperated glance at her. "It's late and you know the rule, one make-believe story per night. Which story did I tell last time?"

"Emma's," Derek said.

"Mine," Emma reluctantly admitted.

"Then it's Derek's turn." He gave Emma a hug meant to console her. "I'll tell the princess story tomorrow."

"Okay," she said in a long-suffering tone. "I'll wait until then."

"That's my girl," he praised. "Let's see, how does it start again?"

"Once upon a time," Derek prompted.

"Ah, yes. Once upon a time there was a young knight who was left in charge of his parents' castle while they went to visit the king. It would be a long journey so to help the knight, the baron and his wife left behind two trusty advisors to guide the young man in case problems should arise."

Christy listened to the story unfold, finding herself as riveted as the children. He'd just reached the part about the baron's son finding a wounded doe when his cell phone jangled.

His warm tone disappeared as he took the call and his professional persona became fully evident. She hoped the reason for the interruption was minor, but when he clicked off his phone, she sensed their family interlude had ended.

"I have to go, kiddos," he apologized affectionately. "So I'll finish the story with 'To be continued'."

Apparently this wasn't the first time a story had been cut short under similar circumstances because the children didn't argue. They simply flung their arms around his neck and kissed him. "'Night, Uncle Linc," they chimed in unison before they slid off his lap. "See you in the morning."

As soon as the two disappeared down the hall, Christy asked, "Problems, I take it?"

He nodded. "Jose is having severe pain in his other leg. I don't know how long I'll be."

That wasn't good news. In spite of being heavily dosed on blood thinners, Jose could still be developing blood clots.

"I didn't realize you were on call."

"I'm not, but Jose asked for me."

Which meant he wouldn't refuse to go to the

hospital, she realized. "I hope everything goes okay for him."

His eyes seemed uncommonly tired as he paused in his path to the door. "Me, too."

Christy hated that his already long day had just been extended. She made a mental note to keep the children as quiet as mice tomorrow morning so he could sleep late. In any case, who would have thought Gail's scenario would have played out so soon? As much as she would have liked to split the parenting duties, sharing them was turning out to be for the best.

As she'd predicted earlier, both Derek and Emma had fallen asleep almost immediately after she'd tucked them in and kissed them goodnight.

She was ready for bed herself, but she and Linc hadn't discussed their sleeping arrangements. Commandeering the master bedroom on her own seemed presumptuous on her part. Although the luxury of Gail and Ty's king-sized bed was enticing, her sense of fair play dictated that Linc deserved the perk. His tall frame would fit so much better there than on the daybed in the guest bedroom. His late and/or early comings and goings would disrupt the household less if he had immediate access to a private bathroom.

Christy turned down her bed, unpacked her clothes, lined her bottles of pills and vitamins on the top of her dresser next to her doctors' appointments cards, tidied the kitchen and let Ria out for her last toilet break of the evening. An hour had passed and Linc still hadn't returned.

She patted on her weekly facial mask, took a long, leisurely shower, slipped on her pink breast cancer awareness Minnie Mouse sleep shirt, then slathered on body moisturizer while Ria watched from her spot on the floor.

Still no Linc.

Afraid that poor Jose was in serious shape, she decided to wait for news. She convinced Ria to lie on her pallet in the living room, then curled up in the easy chair Linc had vacated earlier with one of the paperback books she'd brought from her personal library.

She didn't realize she'd begun dozing until Ria's low grumble startled her awake. As soon as the back door opened, her pet bolted upright and dashed into the kitchen like an enthusiastic puppy rather than a fierce protector.

Clearly, Linc was home.

She padded after her to find Linc rummaging

in freezer for ice. Stifling her yawn, she asked, "How did things go?"

"Good." He filled his plastic tumbler with water and took a long swig of his drink.

"What happened?"

"Jose developed a DVT in his other leg."

She translated his shorthand into "deep vein thrombosis", which shouldn't have happened given all the medication they'd given him earlier in the day. "And?"

"I called in Howard Manning and he inserted a Greenfield filter into his vena cava to stop the clot from entering his lung."

"How's he doing?"

"Fine for now. He'll be monitored closely for a while."

Christy noted the lines of exhaustion on his face and his weary-looking gaze when he glanced at her. While her shirt was perfectly modest and covered as much of her body as regular clothing, she was quite aware they were still only pajamas.

"You should be asleep," he said as he finished off the drink.

"I think I was."

"You didn't have to stay up."

"I wanted to hear about Jose. I also didn't want

Ria to think you were a burglar and sound the alarm, but she obviously knew who you were because she didn't."

As if aware of the hour and disappointed by the lack of attention his humans were paying her, the dog gave a wide, noisy yawn, then turned around and headed for her rug.

"I also couldn't go to bed because we hadn't worked out our sleeping arrangements. I was afraid you'd either stumble around and wake everyone or spend the night in a chair."

"Right now, a chair sounds like heaven."

"Well, there's a bed waiting for you." Aware of how suggestive her comment sounded, she hurried to explain. "I took the spare room. The master bedroom is all yours."

He rubbed his eyes as he nodded. "I should be chivalrous and argue, but maybe tomorrow when I'm not beat."

"Argue all you want, but I've already unpacked my stuff. Do you have to go in early or can you sleep late?"

His smile was small and lopsided. "It's my weekend off, so I don't need an alarm clock."

"Then I'll keep the kids extra-quiet while we eat breakfast."

"It's not necessary. A few hours and I'll be good as new. Wake me in time to help."

"Okay," she said, only because she didn't want to argue with him at two a.m. At some point they would have to discuss job duties and meal planning, but not now. "Will you go to the hospital this weekend to check on Jose?"

He nodded. "I'll drop by late morning or early afternoon."

She knew he wasn't on call this weekend, which made her curious about his plans. "Do you give all of your patients the royal treatment? I don't think any of them would fault you for taking a night or a weekend off and passing their care off to one of your partners."

He refilled his tumbler and drank deeply again. "Probably not, but Jose isn't just a patient. I've known him and his wife for about five years."

"As a patient?"

He shook his head. "I met him when I hired him to build an outdoor fireplace. Because he was eager for the job, he'd work on evenings and weekends when I was at home, and his wife sent along some of her cooking." He grinned. "I think she used me to clean out her leftovers, but I didn't mind. Everything was delicious. Eventually, I got to know their family and when the oldest son expressed an interest in medicine, Jose asked if Emilio could job-shadow me for a week before he started college."

"And you did," she guessed.

He chuckled. "Yeah. Now he's in his final year of medical school." A note of pride filled his voice.

She was half-surprised by his story, and yet, after seeing him interact with his niece and nephew, she wasn't. Obviously he was a completely different person around the people who'd been lucky enough to enter his charmed circle of friends and family. Oddly enough, she realized that she wanted to be included.

Not because she had any romantic designs on him, she hastened to tell herself. Even if her ex, Jon, hadn't blasted the stars out of her eyes, getting that close to a guy wouldn't happen before she got the all-clear on her five-year check-up. It would take someone special to deal with the baggage she carried and she honestly didn't think there was a man alive who could.

"Does he know about his father?"

"I called him this evening. Francesca was too rattled to make sense and I knew Emilio would have a lot of questions." Suddenly he yawned. "Sorry about that."

Immediately, she felt guilty for keeping him from his well-deserved and much-needed sleep. "I'm the one who's sorry. If I hadn't stayed up to ask about Jose, you'd already be in bed asleep. So, go on." She made a shooing motion. "I'll get the lights and lock up."

"Okay, but in the morning you and I need to sort out a few details," he began.

"I'll be here," she promised. Then, looking around, she asked, "Where's your suitcase?"

He snapped his fingers. "I left my duffel bag in the car."

"I'll get it while you hop in the shower."

She expected him to argue, but he simply nodded. "Thanks. It's on the back seat."

When she returned with his bag in hand, she was surprised to hear dead silence. She knocked softly on the master bedroom's door and when she didn't hear an answer, she assumed it was safe to enter.

However, as she peeked inside, she found him lying fully clothed on top of the king-sized bed.

She wanted to wake him so he could change into something more comfortable than his dress clothes and crawl under the covers, but the lines of exhaustion on his face stopped her. The medical residents she'd encountered during her nursing career had learned to fall asleep as soon as they were horizontal, regardless of what they were wearing, and Linc obviously hadn't given up those old habits.

Knowing she couldn't leave him as he was, she tugged off his shoes and placed them side by side on the floor beside his bag. Determined to protect his rest as much as she could, she reassured herself the curtains were tightly pulled and the alarm clock was turned off. By the time she tiptoed to the door and flicked off the overhead light, an occasional soft snore punctuated the silence.

She smiled. Until now, she would have sworn that a man as tightly in control as Linc was wouldn't allow his body to do anything as ordinary as snore. It would be interesting to see how many of her other preconceived opinions he'd disprove over the coming weeks, although she hoped he wouldn't.

Learning that Lincoln Maguire was a great guy underneath his staid exterior would only lead to heartbreak.

* * *

Linc woke to the most delicious aroma—coffee. He sniffed the air again, trying to catalog the other scent that mingled with his beloved caffeinated breakfast blend. It reminded him of...

Waffles. His eyes popped open and it took him a few seconds to realize he wasn't in his own bed. Memories of last night crashed down and he immediately checked the bedside alarm clock.

Eleven-thirty. No wonder the sun was peeking around the edges of the heavy drapes. He couldn't remember the last time he'd slept that late, although he vaguely remembered waking at one point to use the bathroom and shed his clothes before he crawled between cool, fresh-smelling sheets.

He also didn't recall the last time he'd awakened to the aroma of a delicious meal. Although he didn't expect her to prepare his breakfast, he hoped she'd prepared extra for him this morning. As he swung his bare legs over the bed's edge, his stomach rumbled in agreement.

Raking a hand through his hair, he rose, stepped into his previously discarded pants, and followed his nose.

Derek and Emma were seated at the kitchen table and Christy stood in front of the stove, clad in a pair of above-the-knee light blue plaid cotton shorts that showed off her delightfully long legs and a matching blue button-down shirt. Both children had powdered sugar dusting their faces, syrup smeared around their mouths and milk mustaches.

Emma saw him and her eyes lit up. "Christy?" she asked in a loud whisper. "Can we use our regular voices now?"

"Not until you're uncle is awake," she whispered back.

"But he is," she declared in a normal tone. "Morning, Unca Linc."

Christy turned, spatula in hand, and her eyes widened before a big smile crossed her face. "Good morning," she said as her gaze pointedly remained above his neck. "The coffee's ready if you are."

He nearly smiled at her discomfiture, then decided it wouldn't win him any brownie points. "You read my mind. Thanks. Can I pour you a cup, too?"

She shook her head. "I'm not a coffee drinker."

"Really?" he asked as he poured his own mug. "I thought everyone who worked in the medical profession mainlined the stuff."

"I used to, but I switched to herbal tea. It's better for you."

"Probably, but you can't beat a bracing cup of coffee to jump-start the day." He watched her flip a perfectly made waffle out of the iron and dust it with powdered sugar. "That smells good."

She chuckled. "Are you hinting you'd like one?"

He was practically drooling, but he was too conscious of his morning scruffiness to agree. His face itched, he needed a shave and a shower, and his teeth felt furry. He definitely wasn't presentable for the dining table.

"I should clean up first."

"Probably," she agreed, "but this waffle is ready and the griddle's still hot if you'd like seconds." Her gaze traveled up and down his full length, making him even more aware of his half-dressed appearance. "Judging from the way you look, the kitchen will be closed before you come back, so I suggest you eat first and shower later."

He got the sneaking impression that once she unplugged the waffle iron she wouldn't plug it in again. How had he ever thought her easygoing and malleable? She had a steely spine that he'd never seen and certainly hadn't expected.

"I should put on a shirt," he began.

Once again, she avoided his gaze. "Suit yourself, but, whatever you do, I promise to sit downwind."

"Mom never lets Dad eat at the table without a shirt," Derek said, "but if Uncle Linc can, can I?"

This time Christy looked at him helplessly, her gaze sliding from his pectorals to his face and back again. "Well," she began, "these are extenuating circumstances—"

"If those are your mom's rules, then they'll be ours, too," Linc said firmly. "I'll be right back."

The lure of the waffle was too great and the slices of ham too appetizing to do more than grab yesterday's wrinkled shirt and slip it on. He'd only buttoned the middle two buttons before he was back in the kitchen and sliding into an empty chair.

If Christy noticed his speedy return, she didn't comment. Instead, she simply set his plate in front of him, passed the meat platter and returned to the stove.

Linc dug in. He was hungry enough to be grateful for the hospital's bland cafeteria food, but he was pleasantly surprised to discover Christy's meal actually melted in his mouth. When she delivered a second waffle as perfect as the first one, he could only utter a long sigh of appreciation.

"These are delicious," he said as he drenched it with maple syrup.

"Surprised?" She took the chair beside him and began sectioning her grapefruit.

"A little," he admitted. "Where did you learn to cook like this?"

"My mom. She owns an exclusive little gourmet restaurant in Seattle and she sends recipes for me to try before she adds them to her menu."

"Then that explains all the fancy food in the fridge."

Confusion spread across her face. "Fancy food?"

"You know. The organic milk, the fruit and vegetables I can't identify."

She smiled. "I don't consider organic food as being fancy. As for the unidentifiable stuff, I try new things to see if I'll like them." She motioned to his plate. "Speaking of new things, how would you rate this recipe?"

"It's a keeper." The cuckoo suddenly popped out of his door and chirped twelve times. "I didn't realize it was noon. Did you guys sleep late, too?" he asked.

"We've been up for *hours*." Derek drained his

milk glass and wiped his mouth with his forearm until Christy cleared her throat and he sheepishly swiped at it with his napkin.

"Hours and *hours*," Emma added. "Christy said we had to be quiet, so we ate our breakfast on the patio."

"Isn't this breakfast?" he asked.

"This is lunch," Christy corrected. "Breakfast was at eight and consisted of cold cereal, fresh strawberries, pineapple, and toast."

"Whole wheat," Derek mumbled with disgust.

She chuckled and Linc was entranced by the sound. "With all the jelly you slathered on, you couldn't taste or see that I didn't use white bread."

Emma obviously didn't care because she continued her play-by-play account of the morning. "Then we took Ria for a walk around the block so he could get 'quainted with the dog smells in the neighborhood. After that, we watered Mama's flowers and weeded and before we knew it, Christy said it was time to eat again. I think she's almost as good a cook as Mama is, don't you?"

He'd been put on the spot by a mere six-year-old. No matter how he answered, he was going to have one female in the household unhappy. Christy obviously saw his dilemma because her eyes twinkled with humor. He wouldn't receive any help from that quarter....

"Almost," he agreed loyally, as he exchanged a smile with Christy that said otherwise.

"We'll wait for you in the cafeteria," Christy told Linc a few hours later as he parked in the physicians' parking lot. They'd decided to spend the afternoon running errands, including driving to his house to pick up a few of what he referred to as "necessities", but on the way he'd wanted to run in and check on Jose.

"I won't be long, I promise."

"Yeah, right," she said, unable to hide her skepticism.

"You don't believe I can get away in a reasonable amount of time?"

"Only if you went incognito," she said.

"I thought I was," he said. "No one will expect to see me looking like this."

"Like this" meant dressed in a polo shirt, cargo shorts, and a pair of sandals. It wasn't his usual garb, so he'd cause quite a stir when the staff saw him. She spoke from experience because she still couldn't believe this was the same man who'd sat at the kitchen table a few hours ago looking scruffy and bleary-eyed.

A little water and a shave could do amazing things.

As great as he looked now, though, her first image of him was indelibly etched in her brain. His muscles had flexed and rippled under his skin just from the simple act of pouring his own cup of coffee. As much as she'd enjoyed seeing those wide shoulders as nature intended, it was a good thing Derek had piped up when he had. She might have done something really stupid, like set off the smoke alarm or drool in her grapefruit.

Nope, if more women saw the sight she'd been privileged to see, cardiology offices would be standing room only.

"They won't, but if you're going to be longer than thirty minutes, give me a call, will you?"

"Okay, but, whatever you do, don't load them up with a bunch of sugar and junk food."

She paused, momentarily hurt by his remark. "Do you honestly think I'll turn them loose at the candy machine?"

He shifted uncomfortably in the seat. "I think you'd spoil them if you had the chance," he began slowly.

"And you wouldn't, I suppose."

"Once in a while, I do," he admitted, "but—"

Aware of two sets of little ears in the back seat, she lowered her voice and clenched her fingers into a tight fist as she interrupted, "But you think I'll do it all the time."

"Maybe not all—"

"Why else would you remind me?"

He shut off the engine, then gripped the steering wheel with both hands. "I only meant—"

She cut him off once again. "I know what you meant." She didn't know why his lack of faith bothered her, but it did. Yes, they'd only been joint parents for less than twenty-four hours, but where had he gotten the idea she'd let Emma and Derek run amok, nutrition-wise? And if he thought she'd turn a blind eye to their eating habits, what did he think she'd do when making other decisions?

"All I can say is, if you're that worried, you'd better finish your business as quickly as possible so you can supervise what they choose for a snack," she said stiffly.

"I am *not* worried," he said.

"You are, so you may as well admit it." As she turned to face the children, she pasted on a smile and injected a lighter note into her voice. "Okay, gang. Let's go!"

While the two scrambled out of their seat belts, he grabbed her arm. "I'm not worried," he repeated.

"Of course not," she said politely. "My mistake." Then, shaking free, she hopped out of the car and herded her two charges into the hospital like an overprotective mother hen.

When she directed them to the stairwell, Derek complained, "Can't we take the elevator? Uncle Linc is."

"We'll take it on the way up," she prevaricated, unwilling to see for herself or admit that sharing such close confines at the moment was more than she could handle.

With luck, an hour or so of mindlessly watching the fish swim around the aquarium would restore her good mood.

Linc had major damage control facing him. For a man who was normally efficient at stating his thoughts, he'd missed the mark today. He'd hurt Christy with his thoughtless remark—that had been evident and he deeply regretted doing so.

To make matters worse, in trying to explain,

he'd practically told her that she was a pushover when it came to Derek and Emma and he knew she wasn't. Christy's mere glance this morning had convinced Derek to use his napkin instead of his sleeve and if she could do that, she'd be immune to any cajolery they might try.

He checked Jose's chart and slipped into his room to visit for about fifteen minutes. Satisfied by his progress, he strode toward the bank of elevators, ready to leave. As he punched the "Down" button, he wondered if he should kill time elsewhere in the hospital. If he arrived in the cafeteria too soon, Christy would assume he'd hurried to check on her.

The point was he *was* in a hurry, but not for that particular reason. If anyone saw him, he could easily get embroiled in a patient case and he had too many other things to do this afternoon— *family* things—that wouldn't allow it. His objective also included getting to know Gail's best friend because there seemed to be more to her than had previously met his eye.

On the other hand, Christy seemed like a forgiving sort, so perhaps during their time apart she'd decided to cut him some slack.

He strode into the near-empty cafeteria and saw

Emma and Derek peering into the giant aquarium in the far corner of the dining hall.

"Hi, guys. Are you enjoying the fish?" he asked.

"I like the spotted ones," Emma declared as she pointed to one. "Do you know what kind of fish he is?"

Linc referred to the chart posted above the aquarium. "A Dalmation Molly."

Emma giggled. "She looks like a fire-truck dog, doesn't she?"

"She does," he agreed, then asked, "Where's Christy?"

"She's over there with that guy." Derek inclined his head in her direction.

Linc glanced at the corner in question and saw her with a fellow he recognized as one of the physical therapists. From their wide smiles and the laughter drifting across the room, both appeared entirely too comfortable with each other for Linc's taste.

"He's got the hots for her," Derek said with a typical eight-year-old boy's disgust.

Linc had arrived at the same conclusion and was instantly envious. His reaction was completely illogical, but when he saw the guy scoot his chair closer and fling his arm over her shoulder to draw her close enough to whisper in her ear, he felt an envy he hadn't noticed before.

"See?" Derek said with satisfaction. "Maybe we should warn Christy that he wants to get in her—"

Derek's blunt description finally registered and Linc cut off the boy's sentence. "Whoa there, buddy. Does your mother know you're a teenager in an eight-year-old body?"

A blush crept across Derek's face, which suggested his mother probably didn't know the extent of her son's education. "I watch TV," he defended.

"Really?" Linc raised an eyebrow. "Before I ask what sort of programs you're viewing and if your mother knows you are, we aren't going to say a word to Christy. We don't want to embarrass her."

He, on the other hand, was jealous.

The boy shrugged. "If you say so, but it's still true. He held out her chair for her, got her a refill, and keeps putting his arm around the back of her chair and leaning in close. I think he might be her boyfriend."

A boyfriend. Linc hadn't considered the possibility that Christy might have her own reasons for not wanting to share the house with him. Living under someone else's roof with another guy, no matter how innocent it might be, could certainly strain a relationship.

On the other hand, although he didn't socialize with the staff, he'd picked up enough tidbits from conversations around him to know the gossip currently circulating on the grapevine. He'd never heard her name linked to anyone else's. If he had, he would have remembered.

On the other hand, her relationship might be new enough that it hadn't become the latest news yet. Or, as Derek had said, this Masterson fellow might still be trying—

"He isn't," Emma interrupted with childlike certainty.

Linc's mind was too focused on Derek's report of Masterson's activities to follow Emma's train of thought. "He isn't what?"

"Her boyfriend. I heard Mama telling her that she needs to get one, but Christy only laughed and said she'd think about it after her next pet. Do you think she's going to get another dog? I hope she finds a little one next time. One you can carry in your purse."

Linc was totally confused. A boyfriend was

contingent on Christy's new pet? Emma had obviously missed a few important details.

"How long ago did you hear your Mom and Christy talking?" he asked. If their conversation had taken place months ago, Christy could easily have found someone since then to play that role, new pet or not.

"A few days before Mama and Daddy left. Oh, look." Once again, she pointed to the tank. "Those two fish are *kissing.*" She giggled.

He glanced at the tank and saw two fish with their mouths pressed together. The fish clearly didn't spend their days swimming aimlessly around their environment. Once again, he referred to the posted list of names and photos.

"They're called Kissing Gourami," he reported.

"Do you think they like each other, Unca Linc?" Emma asked.

"Don't be silly." Derek rolled his eyes. "Fish don't like each other like people do."

"How do you know?" Emma's eyes flashed. "You don't know everything just 'cause you're older than me. If it's a boy fish and a girl fish, they could, *too,* like each other—"

"Enough," Linc said firmly. "We aren't going

to argue here. We'll research the subject on the internet when we get home."

To his surprise and delight, Christy joined them at the tank. "Actually, those two aren't getting along right now," she said.

"They aren't? But they're acting like they do," Emma protested.

"They're a peaceful species, but the males fight over their territory like other animals. When they do, they press their mouths together."

The little girl frowned as if trying to puzzle over how such a move could be a sign of aggression. "They don't have much room to fight over," she remarked, her attention riveted to the pair in question.

"I don't know how large they consider their territories," Christy replied. "Maybe one raced the other to the food and he was a sore loser. Or maybe one cut in front of the other while they were swimming."

"I get it," Linc said, humored by her story. "They're having the aquatic equivalent of road rage. And I thought I had an active imagination."

Emma tugged on his shorts pocket. "What's road rage?"

"It's when one driver gets angry with another driver and they get into an argument."

"Oh."

"The point is, Em," Christy interrupted, "it doesn't take much for guys of any species to find a reason to flex their muscles."

He had a feeling she'd directed her last comment to him.

"Yeah, but they fight by kissing?" Derek shuddered. "Yuck."

Christy grinned. "You don't like the idea of locking lips with the guy you want to punch?"

"No way."

While Derek and Christy discussed the more acceptable forms of dealing with conflict, Linc realized that her former companion had disappeared. "Is Masterson's coffee break over?"

"Dan had only stopped in for his usual afternoon soda and ran into us. He's on the *Dancing with the Docs* committee and was trying to convince me to volunteer."

"Did he? Convince you, that is?"

She shook her head. "I told him my days were full enough as it is with being a participant, but I'd save him a dance."

Linc felt an unreasonable desire to remind her

that she would be busy dancing with *him*, but he didn't. He did, however, make a mental note to carve out time for lessons the week after next. By then, his partners would have returned from their respective vacations and he could implement a less hectic schedule in the weeks ahead.

"As enjoyable as it is to stay and chat about the fish or the upcoming festival, we have plenty to see and do today," she said.

"You're right. We should leave," he agreed. After tossing the empty cracker wrappers and milk cartons into a bin, Linc ushered the group to the elevator. As they were making their ascent, curiosity drove him to ask, "Emma said you might be getting another dog?"

She smiled. "Afraid not. Ria is all I can handle for now." She touched her finger to the tip of the little girl's nose. "Whatever gave you that idea, Em?"

"We were wondering if that guy you were with was your boyfriend. I said he wasn't 'cause you told Mama you'd get one after your next pet and you still just have Ria."

Linc had expected her to laugh in her usual melodic way—the way that made him smile whenever he heard the sound. He wasn't prepared to see her face turn pale and her hand shake as she touched her throat.

Something had driven the color out of her face. He didn't understand what, but he intended to find out.

CHAPTER FOUR

CHRISTY tried to remember the details of her conversation with Gail and wondered how much Emma had heard. She opted to pretend ignorance. "Trust me. I don't intend to replace Ria or give her a doggy brother or sister. Okay?"

"Then you won't ever have a boyfriend?"

Emma had no idea how painful her innocent question was. "Someday. If I find the right guy," Christy answered lightly, although she had her doubts. In her experience, the good ones were already taken.

Suddenly aware of Linc's speculative gaze, she wondered why the elevator suddenly slowed to a crawl. "I'm too busy for a fella right now anyway." She brushed a lock of unruly hair off Emma's forehead. "I'm looking after my favorite kids, remember?"

Fortunately, they'd arrived on the main floor at that particular moment. As soon as the stainless-steel doors opened, she edged her way through the space so fast she was the first one out.

"What's next on our agenda?" she asked, hoping Linc hadn't noticed her too-bright tone. A quick glance showed an impassive expression so she relaxed, certain she'd successfully dodged that uncomfortable situation.

"My place," he said.

It came as no surprise that Linc lived in an upper-middle-class neighborhood. His sprawling, ranch-style house stood in the middle of a well-manicured lawn. Hostas and other shade-loving perennials circled the large maple trees and a mixture of petunias, marigolds, and other annuals she didn't recognize filled the flower bed next to the front entrance.

"When do you find the time to work outdoors?" she asked as they walked inside.

"I have a yard service," he confessed. "I also have a housekeeper who drops in every three weeks, although there isn't much for her to do."

She didn't expect there would be. The man spent most of his life at the hospital.

"Can we go to the back yard and play, Uncle Linc?" Derek asked.

"Sure," he told them, "but don't get too involved because we won't be staying long."

"Okay." The children scampered through the house and a few seconds later an unseen door slammed.

"What are we getting?" Christy asked, trying not to be awed by his house and failing. The home was built with an open floor plan similar to hers, but his living room also had a gorgeous red-brick fireplace in one corner. His décor included a lot of woodwork and deep accent colors in blues, greens, and browns, which gave a very relaxing atmosphere.

"My single-cup coffeemaker," he said as he skirted the island on his way to the end of the counter where the appliance in question was located. "You don't drink coffee, so it seems a waste to make an entire pot for the one cup I drink on my way to the office."

"True." She glanced around again. "This is absolutely lovely."

"You like it?" he asked.

"Very much. If I lived here, I'd have a tough time leaving to go to work."

She heard childish laughter and screams of delight, so she moved to the French doors that opened onto the patio. There, she looked outside into the most beautiful back yard she could imagine.

An outdoor fireplace and a bricked-in grill formed the wall on the west side of the patio and protected the table and chairs from the setting sun. On the east side, a couple of cushioned lounge chairs were grouped together with a small end table in between.

Beyond that, a pair of large oak trees stood like sentinels in the fenced yard. A tree house was nestled in one and a tire swing hung from a huge branch in the other. A gym with a climbing rope and a slide stood off to one side and both Emma and Derek were crawling over it like agile monkeys.

"This is fantastic!" she exclaimed. "Did you or a previous owner create all this?"

He joined her at the door, his smile wide with well-deserved pride. "Ty and Jose did most of the physical labor, but I helped."

"It's amazing," she remarked, awed by his thoughtfulness for his niece and nephew. She was also extremely aware of his proximity as she could almost feel the heat radiating off his body and the most delightful masculine scent surrounded her. "I suppose you don't call this 'spoiling' your niece and nephew?"

He shook his head. "I call it self-preservation. Gail and Ty always designate one night a month as their date night, so I began hosting sleepovers at my place. Sometimes they stretched into a full weekend. After one visit of hearing 'We're bored, Unca Linc,' and 'Can we go to the park and play on the swings' every five minutes, I decided it would be easier on all of us if they had something special to play on here. So I commissioned everything you see."

"I'm very impressed." And she was. He might be single-minded about his work, but he didn't completely ignore his family, as she'd first thought.

"Impressed enough to forgive me for my comment this afternoon?"

She had to think a minute to remember. "Oh, that. I'd already forgotten."

"Really?" he asked. "You were rather upset."

She shrugged. "At the time I was. As a general rule, I try to look at what happened in terms of the big picture and usually nothing is so bad that it's worth making a fuss about. Although it takes me a bit longer to reach that point when my feelings are hurt, eventually I get there."

"That's a very healthy attitude to have."

Facing one's mortality had a tendency to change one's perspective. "Thanks."

"I didn't mean to hurt your feelings."

She fell silent. "I accept your apology, but the question is do you trust me to exercise good judgment with Derek and Emma? If you don't, I'd like to know now."

"I don't *distrust* you," he said slowly. "Old habits simply die hard and as the responsible person in my family, it seemed like I was always reminding my siblings to do one thing or another. My parents left me in charge a lot, and by the time they died, it had become second nature. 'Don't forget your lunch money. Pick up a loaf of bread on your way home from school. Start the laundry when you get home.'"

"Ah, the controlling type."

"If by controlling you mean trying to keep everything organized and running smoothly, then yes."

"I'm surprised you took on that responsibility by yourself."

He grinned. "I did, and I didn't. My grandmother was still alive and she wanted Ty and Joanie to move in with her, but Gram was already showing signs of senile dementia and had a heart problem. Taking care of two teenagers would have completely done her in. The three of us voted to move her in with us. She felt useful and we unobtrusively kept an eye on her."

"That's amazing."

He shrugged. "It was the best solution at the time and in hindsight I'm glad we made that decision because a year later she died in her sleep."

"I'm sorry," she murmured.

"She was a great gal. She tended to deliver last-minute instructions every time anyone left the house—young or old, it didn't matter—and I suppose I picked up that habit early on."

"How did Ty and your sister handle those *little reminders*?"

"We had our moments, but they listened." His grin was a beautiful sight to see. "Or at least they pretended to listen."

"So is that what I should do?" she teased. "Pretend to hang on your every word until your ego can't fit through doorways?"

"It's a pleasant thought, but I'd rather have honesty."

"Honesty I can do."

As they exchanged a smile, she felt as if they'd

reached a milestone. Sharing the responsibility of the children didn't seem quite as frustrating as she'd once thought. Maybe, just maybe, they could get through the next two months without feeling as if she were tiptoeing through a minefield.

Oh, they were certain to clash; it was inevitable because he was the type of man who grabbed the horns of leadership. He was used to being the guy with the answers and had been for most of his life. Becoming a surgeon had only reinforced his independence. To him, decisions weren't by group consensus and consequently he expected people to follow his directives without question.

She, on the other hand, believed in hearing both sides and weighing all the pros and cons before arriving at a solution. To her, flexibility and family relationships were far more important than schedules and to-do lists. Life was simply too precarious not to enjoy it to the fullest.

"I'll try to be more sparing with my reminders," he added, "but in case I forget, don't take them personally."

"Okay, as long as you understand I don't handle 'control' very easily."

He chuckled. "I suspected as much. Now that

we've cleared the air, we should discuss our free time."

"Free time?"

"Yeah. If you ever want to go out with Masterson—"

"I don't," she said firmly. "He's a great guy, but…" she wasn't ready to bare her soul, so she relied on her standby excuse "…the sparks aren't there."

"Are you sure? He certainly has them."

"Were you *spying* on me?"

He held up his hands. "I'm only repeating what Derek said."

The knowledge that an eight-year-old boy saw the very fire she'd been trying to extinguish was disconcerting.

"The point is, whether you want to go out with him or anyone else, I'm sure Gail and Ty don't expect either of us to forego dating for the next two months. We need to create a schedule."

Another schedule. How in the world did the man keep track of them all? She pictured his daily calendar and imagined a block of time designated as 'Christy's date', and inwardly smiled.

She didn't know if he was fishing or being kind, but admitting she didn't have a romantic inter-

est and only went out with her girlfriends or colleagues for an occasional beer at the end of a long
week made her seem…sad and pathetic. She'd endured enough of people's well-meant sympathy
over the past four-plus years and she especially
didn't want any from Lincoln Maguire.

"Your suggestion is noted," she said instead.
"I'll give you plenty of notice when I have plans.
What about you? Is there a lady friend in your
life that I should work around?"

"Not really. I have met someone, though. No, I
take that back. We've been passing acquaintances
for a while, but lately I'm seeing her a little differently."

The idea that another woman had attracted his
attention was unsettling, which was a completely
illogical response. Just because her pulse did that
stupid skittery thing when he was around and
just because they were living together under the
most innocent of terms for the sake of two minors
didn't mean she had a right to be possessive. A
man who thrived on control and preferred having
everything in its place wouldn't be interested in
a woman who walked a tightrope between being
cured of cancer and having a relapse.

"Anyone I know?" she asked, realizing her off-handed question was as painful as poking herself in the eye.

"I'd rather not name names at this point."

She didn't know what was worse—knowing the woman's identity or being left to speculate. "Okay, but if you ever ask her out—"

"You'll be the first to know."

His promise brought little comfort because the green-eyed monster had perched on her shoulder.

Linc had hoped Christy would be more forthcoming about her personal life when he'd mentioned creating a date-night schedule, but she hadn't. Hearing she didn't feel the sparks with Masterson had come as some relief, but Masterson wasn't the only guy sniffing around her. She attracted single fellows like grape jelly attracted orioles, although, as far as he could tell, she didn't encourage them.

No doubt they responded to her ready smile and open friendliness, which he completely understood. He lingered longer on her nursing unit than he did elsewhere in the hospital because lately, even if he only spent a few minutes with her and they never discussed anything except patient care, being with her seemed to rejuvenate him.

It was an odd observation. She was unconventional and impulsive—two traits he hadn't been looking for in his ideal significant other because he wasn't about to have *his* children live through the same upheaval and uncertainty he had—but apparently, like the other eligible males in the hospital, he was drawn to her because of them.

For the first time he began to wonder if steady and dependable was really what he wanted. After all, he'd met a multitude of steady, dependable women and yet he hadn't bothered to get to know any of them. Was it possible that deep down, in spite of his avowal otherwise, he wanted the excitement that his parents had enjoyed as they'd pursued their dream together?

Maybe he did, but he'd certainly go about achieving it in a different way, and he certainly wouldn't do so by placing an unreasonable burden on his children. Surely there was a happy medium? He simply had to find it.

In the meantime, though, he'd solve the riddle of the "pet" comment Emma had overheard because his instincts said there was more to that particular story than Christy had divulged.

To his surprise, the pieces which hadn't fit suddenly slid into place later that evening.

"Unca Linc, I need you."

Emma's loud whisper pulled his attention away from his latest *Lancet* journal as he sat in the recliner with his feet raised. "What's up, Em?" he asked in a normal voice.

"Shh," she whispered, holding a finger to her lips. "I don't want Christy to hear. I need you. *Now.*" She motioned frantically for him to join her.

The worry on her elfin features convinced him to follow. As soon as he reached her side, she pulled him into the hallway that led to the bed-rooms.

"What's up?" he whispered back.

"I'm in a bit of a pickle," she admitted, "but I can't 'splain yet. Christy will hear."

He smiled at her turn of a phrase because it sounded like something his sister-in-law fre-quently said. "She's outside."

Emma's shoulders heaved. "Oh, good."

"So what's this pickle you're in?" he asked, try-ing to not smile when Emma was clearly dis-tressed.

She stopped outside Christy's room and the story poured out of her. "I know we're not s'posed to go into rooms when we're not invited, but Ria and I were playing and Ria ran in here and I came after her. She was jumping and I was trying to stay out of her way but we both bumped into the dresser and Christy's stuff rolled off and some of the bottles fell off the back and I can't get them out!" Her voice rose. "Now Christy's going to be mad at us and she won't let me play with Ria or talk to Mama and Daddy when they call tonight and I just gotta talk to them! Please, Unca Linc. You hafta help me."

With that, she burst into tears.

Linc's mouth twitched with a smile, but laughing at Emma's worries wouldn't allay his niece's fears. Instead, he crouched down and hugged her.

"None of this is as bad as you think," he consoled, wiping away her tears with his thumbs. "We'll get the bottles and set them back on top of the dresser. No harm done."

Emma sniffled.

"Were they big bottles or little ones?" he asked.

"Little. Mama gets the same ones when she's sick."

She must have knocked over prescription

bottles. "Okay. Give me two minutes and everything will be just like it was."

"But she'll know I came into her room without her permission," she hiccupped, "and then I'll be punished. So will Ria."

The Labrador sat on her haunches next to the bed, her usual doggy smile absent, as if she recognized the gravity of the situation.

"You may get scolded, but Christy wouldn't stop you from talking to your mom and dad."

"You don't think so?" Her watery blue-gray eyes stared into his. "What we did was wrong."

"Yes, it was, but not allowing you to talk to your mom and dad would be mean, and deep down you know she isn't mean." He paused. "Am I right?"

She nodded and the worried wrinkle between her eyes lessened.

"I'll move the dresser, we'll find her things and put them back the way they were. Now, don't cry. Okay?"

She swiped her nose and nodded. "Okay."

Linc pivoted the dresser far enough to locate the missing prescription containers. After retrieving them, he moved the furniture so the legs matched the same carpet depressions as they had previously. Satisfied he'd hidden the evidence of the mishap, he placed the two he'd rescued at the end of the row of her other medications and neatly stacked the appointment cards.

Noticing that she'd positioned each bottle so the labels faced outward, he lined his in the same manner, half-surprised that someone as young and obviously healthy as Christy required so much medication. As he turned away, he caught one drug name out of the corner of his eye and his blood immediately ran cold.

Tamoxifen.

Although he didn't prescribe it for his patients, he knew exactly what it was used for—the treatment of certain types of breast cancer.

The books on her shelf now made sense, as did the row of pill bottles and vitamins, her organic hormone-free milk, and the refrigerator full of fresh vegetables and low-fat dairy products.

It also made her guiding philosophy of life understandable. After battling cancer, there weren't many other problems too big to face and definitely not many worth getting upset over.

But, oh, how he hated to think of what she'd gone through, both physically and emotionally.

"Unca Linc." Emma tugged on his pants. "Are you done? We should go."

"You're right, we should." He ushered her out of the room and closed the door firmly behind him, wishing he could block off his new-found knowledge as easily.

"There you two are," Christy said with relief as she and Derek met Linc and Emma in the living room. "It's almost time for Gail and Ty to call. Linc, can you power up the laptop?"

While he obeyed, she addressed the children. "Let me look at you and make sure you're both presentable."

She stood them side by side and cast a critical eye on them. The clean clothes they'd changed into an hour ago were still clean. Emma's hair was neatly combed, but Derek's definitely needed a bit of straightening. She couldn't do it properly so she simply smoothed the unruly locks with her fingers.

"Gail and Ty aren't expecting them to look their Sunday best," Linc teased her. "They know these two. If they're too neat, Gail will accuse us of replacing her kids with someone else's."

"I don't want them to think we're neglecting—"

"Trust me, they won't. As long as they're not bleeding, a little dirt and stray hair won't faze

Gail and Ty." He pushed a few keys, then set the laptop on the coffee table in front of the youngest Maguires, who were bouncing with excitement on the sofa. "Here we go."

At seven o'clock on the dot, thanks to a wireless internet connection and a webcam, Gail and Ty appeared on the computer screen and the conversation began.

Christy moved into the background and listened as the children talked about their recent activities and Gail mentioned a few of the sights they'd seen. She and Linc gave a short statement about how well things were going and eventually, after a promise for a follow-up call on Thursday and a tearful goodbye, he closed the connection.

"Can we do that again?" Emma asked.

"On Thursday," Christy told her.

"I want to talk before then."

Arranging a time to coordinate with school events, homework, dance lessons, and soccer practice had been tough, so everyone had agreed to plan their calls near the children's bedtime. Unfortunately, with the seven-hour time difference, it meant Gail and Ty they had to call at three a.m. local time, which explained why they'd looked a little bleary-eyed.

"I know you do, but your mom and dad have to wake up in the middle of the night to talk to us. They can't do that every day."

"But I didn't tell Mama about the caterpillar I saw and Daddy doesn't know about my loose tooth."

"I'll help you email them," Linc offered. "How does that sound?"

Emma frowned, her bottom lip quivering as if she wouldn't need much encouragement to break into a wail.

He tugged on the little girl's earlobe. "Did you lose your smile? You'd better find it quick because you'll need it for school tomorrow. You don't want your teacher calling me and saying that Emma Maguire is being grumpy today, do you?"

"No."

"Good. Now, run and get ready for bed." He glanced at Christy. "Whose turn is it tonight? The princess or the knight?"

"The princess," Emma stated firmly. With Linc's one, innocently phrased question, eagerness replaced her downcast expression.

Christy was impressed by the way he'd turned his niece's ill-humor completely around. Was his success born out of experience or did he have an innate gift for handling children? Given his past, she suspected a combination of both were responsible.

"Okay, then. Off you go. The longer it takes you to get ready for bed, the shorter the story will be."

The two dashed off and Christy felt Linc's gaze. "What's wrong?" she asked.

"Nothing. I just wondered if you felt better now."

"I've felt fine all evening," she said, puzzled. "Why?"

"You were as fidgety as the kids. I assumed you were nervous."

She sank onto the sofa, surprised he'd noticed. "I was. I wanted everything perfect so Gail wouldn't worry about them or wonder if they'd made the right decision when they asked me, *us*, to watch them."

"Trust me, she saw two happy, healthy kids who were coping with their parents' absence quite well."

"I'm glad you think so."

"I do."

"Unca Linc!" Derek called from his bedroom. "We're ready!"

Laughing, he rose. "Now, if you'll excuse me, my fans await."

For a few minutes Christy listened to Linc's deep voice as he began his story. She couldn't hear the words, but she heard the tone and it touched her in ways she hadn't expected.

Idly, she wondered how Linc would deal with a diagnosis such as hers if delivered to *his* wife or girlfriend. Would he decide, as Jon had, that he hadn't bought a ticket for that particular movie and wasn't interested in doing so? Or would he see her through the entire process—the surgery, the chemo, more surgery, the endless waiting for test results?

She suspected he wouldn't leave his significant other hanging in similar circumstances. A man who'd taken on the care of his younger siblings as well as his grandmother while barely in his twenties wouldn't walk away from a woman he loved.

On the other hand, after taking on so many responsibilities at such a young age, he obviously wasn't interested in tying himself down because he was in his late thirties and didn't seem interested in changing his marital status. His career *was* both wife and mistress, so imagining him in Jon's place was pointless.

Life was what it was and fate had given her a fellow whose love hadn't been strong enough to face the challenges that had presented themselves. In hindsight, she was grateful to have discovered his character flaws before their relationship had become legal.

As for the future, self-preservation ruled the day. She wouldn't allow any man to get close until she received her five-year all-clear report. Without that medical reassurance, it wouldn't be fair to dump such a heavy burden on a guy. Waiting until then would also save her the trouble of dealing with heartache in addition to cancer, round two.

Aware of the hour, Christy tidied the living room, sent Ria outside for her last trip outdoors, then delivered her own share of goodnight hugs and kisses to Derek and Emma. For some reason, though, when they both turned away to leave Emma's bedside, the little girl clung to Linc and whispered in his ear.

"You should tell her," she heard him say.

"Please?" the little girl begged.

"Okay. I'll do it, but next time you have to 'fess up yourself."

"Thanks, Unca Linc."

Curious about what Emma considered so terrible that her uncle had to divulge it on her behalf, Christy held her questions until she'd called in Ria and they were both relaxing on the living-room sofa with the television volume turned low.

"What couldn't Emma tell me about?" she asked as she sipped on her cup of herbal tea.

"She went into your room today."

Considering all of her medications, vitamins, and supplements, which might pique a child's curiosity, Christy panicked. "She didn't swallow anything, did she? Ria didn't eat—"

"No, nothing like that."

She relaxed. "Good."

"Apparently Emma has this horrible fear you'd be furious if you knew she went into your room. She believes she's facing a fate worse than death and asked me to beg for mercy on her behalf."

Christy smiled at Linc's wry tone. "I told them I had things in my room that could make them or Ria sick, so it would be best if they didn't go inside unless I gave them permission." She didn't intend to explain what those things were; she simply hoped Linc would accept her simplified explanation as the kids had.

"Emma understands that, which was why she was worried."

"Out of curiosity, how did she end up there, anyway?"

"She and Ria were playing and somehow the two of them ended up in your room. In their exuberance, some of the bottles on your dresser rolled off. Nothing broke, so you shouldn't worry about that."

"Then no harm done, I'm sure," she said lightly.

"The problem was," he continued, "a few vials rolled behind and she couldn't reach them."

"Thanks for telling me. I would have wondered why some had disappeared. Before I go to bed I'll—"

"The lost have been found. I put the vials on top of your dresser with the others."

She swallowed hard. "You...did?" Then she plastered a wide smile on her face and pretended nonchalance. "How nice of you. Thanks."

"You're welcome."

At first, she believed she'd skated through that awkward moment with ease, but the compassion she saw on his face said otherwise. He might not ask questions—it would be rather forward of him to do so—but whether he did or didn't, his eyes held a *knowing* look that hadn't been present before.

Of the pills he'd retrieved, only one would have generated the curiosity and sympathy in his gaze—the one easily recognizable as a cancer treatment.

If she didn't say a word, she sensed he'd drop the subject, but it seemed cowardly not to address the obvious. It would become the elephant in the room they both tried to ignore and she would analyze his every remark and every glance for a hidden meaning.

She could handle anything from him except pity.

No, she didn't want that. Better to face the situation head-on.

"You know, don't you?" she asked.

CHAPTER FIVE

YOU know, don't you? Christy's question echoed in Linc's head and he paused to debate the merits of pretending ignorance. However easy it might seem in the moment, honesty had been and always would be the best policy.

Her eyes held resignation, as if she hated that her secret had been revealed, and he softened his own gaze. "I wasn't being curious. I didn't intend to read the label, it just happened."

From the way Christy visibly hunched her shoulders in an effort to draw inside herself, Linc knew he'd thrown her off balance. He had plenty of questions, but there were times to speak and times to listen. At the moment, listening seemed to be the most appropriate course of action.

Had anyone else told him news of this sort, he would have reacted in a most clinical, detached manner. With Christy, however, his detachment had flown out the window.

Sensing her mental turmoil, he scooted closer to lend his comfort and encouragement. She stiffened in his one-armed hug as if she didn't want to accept his support, but gradually the tension in her body eased.

Silence hung in the air as she continued to cradle her teacup, but Linc waited.

"You're probably wondering why I never told you," she began.

"Not really." At her startled glance, he explained. "I'm not your physician or…" He wanted to say *your lover* but caught himself. "Or more than a casual acquaintance, so I understand why you haven't shared your personal issues with me. I assume Gail knows?"

"We hadn't shared too many yoga classes before I told her. One doesn't keep many secrets from the ladies at the gym," she said wryly. "For the record, though, my having breast cancer doesn't diminish my ability to look after Derek and Emma."

"Of course not," he answered quickly, to soothe her obvious fears that somehow he'd find her lacking. It also made sense as to why she'd been so worried about the children's appearance for tonight's internet call and had driven herself frantic to make everything perfect. She wanted to prove she could handle the job.

"Good, because for the time being I'm perfectly healthy."

His mental cogs clicked together. "Then Emma wasn't far off the mark, was she? The pet she'd heard you mention was a PET *scan*, not a four-legged animal."

She nodded, a small smile curving her vulnerable mouth. "Yes. My five-year check-up is due a few days after Gail and Ty return, so you don't have to worry about—"

He snagged onto the time frame she'd divulged. "Five years?"

"I was twenty-four when I was diagnosed, which gives me the dubious honor of being one of those rare young people who develop breast cancer. Mine was a particularly aggressive type, so I opted for a double mastectomy."

Knowing what he did about the drug she was taking, her tumor had also been estrogen-receptor positive, which meant estrogen fueled the cancer. Tamoxifen would stop production of the hormone so the abnormal cells couldn't multiply.

"Speaking from a medical standpoint, you made a wise decision."

She shrugged. "It was the only one I *could* make. Because you're curious, as are most men, all this..." she motioned to her chest "...is courtesy of a skilled plastic surgeon and reconstruction."

Admittedly, he enjoyed seeing those curves and fantasizing about them, but he considered himself more of a leg man. Picturing her long legs and those miles of smooth skin wrapped around his waist was one strong image that would keep him awake at night. "I'm not most men."

She grew thoughtful. "You're not, are you?"

He wasn't sure if she was paying him a compliment or not. "As for worrying about your ability to look after Derek and Emma, I'm not. I merely wanted to say that whatever you need to do, whenever you need to do it, we'll handle the logistics."

"Thanks, but for now I only need to swallow my pills, eat right, and take care of myself, which is what every other person on the planet should do."

"True." Thinking of his upcoming week, he leaned forward. "About the taking-care-of-yourself part, one of my colleagues is still on vacation. I won't be able to pull my share of the load until next weekend so unfortunately you'll have to carry the extra burden. After that, things should settle down considerably."

In light of Christy's revelation, he'd make sure he was available after that. Although he sensed she wouldn't appreciate being treated as gently as if she were blown glass, he'd make a point to stay alert and step in whenever she needed extra help. Gail and Ty really had been smart to ask them to share parenting duties. They'd obviously foreseen areas of potential problems and had prepared for them. Now it was his turn to do the same.

"Thanks for the warning," she said.

"Meanwhile, I don't want you to physically do more than you should. You don't have to be Super-Aunt. No one is holding you to an impossible standard, least of all me."

He'd expected her to appreciate his support, but instead she bristled. "I'm quite capable of taking care of the kids, maintaining the house, and doing my job at the hospital. This is precisely why I don't blurt out my history to everyone I meet. People tend to wrap me in cotton wool and treat me like an invalid, but I'm *not*."

"Of course you aren't," he said, realizing she'd misinterpreted his intent. "I was trying to be con-

siderate. That's all. I don't want you to be afraid
I'll complain if I come home and find dishes in
the sink."

Her hackles seemed to drop. "Sorry. I get a little
defensive sometimes. It really bugs me when I'm
told I can't or shouldn't do something because I
had cancer."

So many things now made sense, from her can-
do, full-steam-ahead attitude to the myriad daring
activities that most people would shun. "Offends
your overdeveloped sense of independence, does
it?"

Color rose in her face. "It does," she admitted.
"That's why…"

When she stopped in midsentence, he filled in
the blanks. "That's why you go skydiving, white-
water rafting, and all the other physically chal-
lenging hobbies you're known for."

Her eyes widened. "How did you know?"

"It was a logical assumption. Anyone trying to
prove themselves usually chooses a task that most
people wouldn't dream of doing."

"I haven't done anything *that* bizarre or unusual," she pointed out. "Lots of people go white-
water rafting."

"Sure, but skydiving?"

"Okay, so that's not quite as popular, but my little excursions are my way to celebrate a good medical report. Some people reward themselves with chocolate. I work on my bucket list."

He was relieved to know she wasn't a thrill-seeker, as he'd thought; she was only working her way through a list of experiences. He instantly felt small for misjudging her motives.

"So what's on tap for this year?" he asked. "Bungee-jumping? Swimming with sharks? Diving for sunken treasure?"

"My list consists of things I want to do before I kick the proverbial bucket, not the things that would kill me in the process," she said wryly. "The first two you mentioned are definitely out, although..." she tapped her mouth with her fore-finger "...the sunken treasure idea has possibili-ties, provided I find time to learn how to scuba dive."

He chuckled. "I stand corrected. So what's left?"

"A trip to Paris. Walking on a glacier. Yodeling in the Swiss Alps. Watching my nieces and neph-ews graduate from college. They're younger than Derek and Emma—my sister has two boys and my brother has two girls and a boy. It'll be a while until I can cross off that entry and I intend to be around until I do."

He smiled at her determination and applauded her for it. "Do they live around here?"

"They live in the Seattle area near my mom. My family wasn't happy when I moved to the Midwest, but they understood."

He suspected she'd relocated as a way to assert her independence. However, it didn't take much imagination to picture the resistance Christy had encountered when she'd announced her plans to leave the bosom of her family. He'd spent weeks trying to convince his own sister to accept the promotion her company had offered here in Levitt Springs, but she'd wanted to strike out on her own, too. He would have preferred having her only fifteen minutes away instead of ninety, but she had to live life on her terms, not his. In the grand scheme of things, however, she was relatively close and he could bridge the distance with a mere hop and a skip.

"Then your family was your support group?" he asked.

"I don't think I would have kept going if not for them and my friends. They drove me to doctors' appointments and chemo sessions when I couldn't, loaded my refrigerator with chicken soup, and took me shopping at Victoria's Secret when my reconstruction was completed. They were the greatest. Everyone should have support like I did."

That explained the scrappy underwear he'd found. Unfortunately, being reminded of her lingerie made him wonder what color she was wearing today.

Yanking his mind off that dead-end track, he noticed one significant absence in her list of supportive people. "Assuming you had a boyfriend, where was he in all this?"

She let out a deep sigh of apparent resignation. As if recognizing her mistress's inner turmoil, Ria padded to the sofa and rested her jaw on Christy's knee. She scratched the dog's ears and met his gaze. "He took off."

He wasn't surprised; he'd seen enough in his own practice to know that some people simply couldn't handle illness, whether it was their own or their spouse's, but the idea of leaving someone under those circumstances was beyond his ability to comprehend.

"What happened?"

"Jon seemed to accept my diagnosis through the

talk of lumpectomies, chemotherapy, losing my hair, et cetera, until the word 'mastectomy' was mentioned. When 'double' was added to the table as the best course of action, even though he knew I planned to undergo reconstruction so I'd have my figure back by Christmas, he freaked out."

"So he left."

"Not immediately. The final straw came when he learned I'd need hormone suppression therapy for at least five years and my ovaries might or might not wake up and be ready to work. He wanted kids of his own, through the usual method and not through special medical means, so he wished me luck, kissed me goodbye, and I never saw or heard from him again."

In his disgust Linc muttered an expletive that would have shocked the most hardened longshoreman.

She burst out laughing, clapping her hands over her mouth as her eyes twinkled the entire time. "My, my, Dr Maguire. I'd scold you for your language but those are my sentiments exactly."

He grinned. "It's nice to know we're on the same page." After a brief hesitation he spoke again. "He's the reason you won't date until your next scan, isn't he?"

"I date," she protested mildly. "Just not often and it's never serious. I make that plain from the beginning."

"Do you explain why?"

She looked at him with a measure of horror. "Of course not. Actually, that's not quite true. I'd gone out with someone before I moved to Levitt Springs two years ago."

Instinctively, he knew this story wouldn't have a happy ending either, but knowledge was power and he wanted the facts so he knew exactly what demons she was fighting. "What happened?"

"Nothing. I shared everything I've told you— maybe not quite *everything*..." her smile was rueful "...but Anthony knew about my cancer and the surgeries. We had a wonderful evening."

She paused and he sensed a "but" was coming.

"After he took me home, I never heard from him again," she finished.

He cursed under his breath and she smiled. "It wasn't that bad," she told him. "We only went out once. When I realized he wouldn't call, I was disappointed but not crushed. After that, I moved here and decided to keep my tale to myself. Some women tell everyone they meet about their cancer experience and I understand why they do. The

more women realize it could happen to them—
at any age—the better, but for me, I want people
to see me for who I am, not for what I've gone
through in the past or might in the future."

"Aren't you selling us short? You shouldn't assume all men are as weak-willed and lacking in
character as those two."

"I know," she admitted, "but I can't take the
risk. If a particular relationship is meant to be,
it'll happen at the right time, under my terms."

He hated that she'd lumped all men in the same
category, himself included. "When did Ria appear on the scene?"

"After Jon disappeared to find the new love of
his life, my brother brought me a puppy. She was
beautiful, happy, and loved the water, so I named
her Ria. She also had the biggest paws, which
made me afraid she was part horse, but in the end
she was my best friend and was there whenever
I needed a warm body to hold on to."

Once again, he had an uncommon urge to hunt
down this Jon character and do him bodily harm.
As special as Ria was, Christy should have had
a real person holding her during those dark days
and nights. In fact, he wished he'd known her at

the time because he couldn't imagine leaving her. A person didn't desert the one he loved.

Yet he was glad this guy had decamped, otherwise *he* might never have met her. The possibility of living the rest of his life without her waltzing into it drove the air out of his lungs like a fist to his solar plexus.

"Now you know my whole sordid tale," she said lightly, "and why fundraising for the cancer center and the Relay for Life organization is important to me."

"You could be the hospital's poster child for the event," he pointed out.

"I could, but I won't. I'll leave that to someone else." She grinned. "I'm going to be too busy getting my dance partner up to speed for the competition."

"Speaking of which, did you have to drag *me* into your plan?" he said in mock complaint.

"I did," she stated innocently, although her eyes sparkled with humor. "You always walk into the unit so completely focused on nursing notes and lab reports that I decided you should get involved on a more personal level."

"I'm involved," he protested mildly. Being conscious of her fragrance and the softness of her skin, he could think of at least one other activity in which he'd like to involve himself. "I write a check and it comes out of my *personal* bank account."

One of her eyebrows arched high. "Writing a check is nice, but it isn't *participation*."

"Well, thanks to you, I'm participating now," he complained good-naturedly.

She giggled. "You are, aren't you?"

While his apprehension about sailing around the floor in front of a group of people hadn't faded, it seemed small and insignificant when compared to Christy's challenges. Spending an evening in the company of a woman who embraced life to the degree that she did wouldn't be the royal pain in the backside that he'd first thought. Perish the thought, but, to borrow her phrase, it would probably be...fun.

"I'm warning you, though. After this week, when I don't have to cover so many extra shifts, we're going to start practicing," he said firmly. "And I do mean *practice*."

A small wrinkle formed between her eyebrows. "I was only teasing about getting my dance partner up to speed."

"You have may have been teasing, but I'm not."

"Need I remind you this is only a friendly event? No one is expecting you to be Patrick Swayze."

"If they are, they'll be sorely disappointed, but if something is worth doing—and you keep telling me it is," he added wryly, "then we're going to do it well."

As he saw her smile, he asked, "What's so funny?"

The grin disappeared, but the humor remained in her eyes. "Nothing," she said innocently. "If you want to practice, we'll practice."

The cuckoo suddenly chirped eleven times, which caught Linc by surprise. He wondered where the hours had gone, but he'd been so engrossed in Christy's story that he hadn't noticed how quickly the evening had passed.

"I'd better start the dishwasher before I forget." She rose out of his loose embrace. "Then I'm turning in."

As he followed suit, his arm felt empty and almost unnatural, as if his body sensed what his mind could not—that she belonged there. Not just for a few minutes or over the course of a conversation, but for years and years.

Perhaps it was time he reconsidered a few points

he'd etched in stone. The ideal woman he'd hoped to find—the one with steady, dependable traits—suddenly didn't seem quite as attractive she had a few weeks ago. Being with Christy had made his nameless, faceless future wife seem so…colorless, so black and white.

He now wanted color in his life.

Out of habit, he checked the front door to be sure the deadbolt was thrown, and armed the alarm system.

It was such a husbandly sort of thing to do, he decided as he waited for her to return so he could turn off the lights. Yes, he knew she could flick the switch as easily as he could, but he'd reverted back to his early days when his family had been together. He had always been the last to go to bed because, as the man of the house, he'd accepted the responsibility of securing their home for the night. Old habits, as he'd told Christy, definitely died hard because he'd fallen back into them as if it were only yesterday.

He heard the water running into the dishwasher, then the rhythmic swish as it circulated, but she still hadn't reappeared. Wondering what had delayed her, he meandered into the kitchen and found her with her hands planted on the counter, head down.

"Is something wrong?" he asked.

She straightened immediately and turned toward him, but he saw the too-forced smile. "Why do you ask?"

"You looked as if you were a few hundred miles away."

Her smile was small. "I suppose I was," she said slowly. "For years I haven't thought about some of the things I shared tonight. I'd pushed Jon and the incident with Anthony completely out of my mind, but remembering the way it was…now my emotions are a little tangled."

He didn't believe she had pushed those two experiences out of her head as much as she thought she had. The fact that she intended to hold any fellow at arm's length until she passed her magical five-year date proved that both men's rejections continued to color her relationships.

"Understandable," he said, "but I'm honored you opened up to me. For the record, though, if you hadn't have volunteered the information, I wouldn't have pressed."

"The story was bound to come out sooner or later. You can't share a house with someone and keep any secrets," she said ruefully. "I trust, though, you'll hold everything in confidence? It's not that I don't want anyone in Levitt Springs to know, but I'd rather tell people in my own time and in my own way."

"I won't say a word."

"Thanks."

He sensed the absence of her normally confident air and he felt somewhat responsible. If he'd pretended ignorance about the pills, denied any knowledge of what he'd seen, she wouldn't be reliving the sting of her ex-boyfriend's rejection.

Impulsively, feeling as if he needed to comfort her as he would a distraught Emma, he covered the distance and drew her against him. "Jon was, and still is, an ass," he murmured against her hair. "For that matter, so is Anthony."

She shook in his arms and he didn't know if she was laughing or crying until she spoke. Then he heard the hoarse, tell-tale quiver in her voice. "They are."

"You're better off without them."

"I am," she agreed.

"Jon definitely didn't deserve you."

"He didn't."

She sounded as if she was repeating the arguments she'd used before. He pulled away just enough so he could tip up her chin and stare into her chocolate-brown eyes. "A fellow with any brains would be happy to call you his, cancer diagnosis or not."

She licked her bottom lip before squeezing out a weak smile. "Thanks for the thought."

His gaze landed on her mouth and he instantly realized she was definitely *not* Emma by any stretch of his imagination. He had an uncontrollable urge to determine if her lips would fit his as well as her body did, and if they tasted as delicious as he suspected. Before he could restrain himself, he bent his head and kissed her.

It was a chaste kiss, one meant to console, but not only did that contact pack a powerful punch, it also ignited a hunger inside him.

Gradually, he increased the pressure, waiting for her to respond to his lead, and to his utter delight she did. He caressed her back, carefully encouraging her to lean closer until he finally felt her weight settle against him. Little by little, he inched one hand toward her bare shoulder. Entranced by the smooth skin, he trailed his fingers along the bones before stopping at the hollow of her throat.

He'd run his fingers along the skin of countless patients, but his touch had been clinical as he'd felt for lumps, bumps, and other signs of illness. This time it was different. This time his sensitive fingertips noticed softness while his nose picked up the fresh, floral scent that was pure Christy.

Stopping was impossible; it seemed crucial to catalogue every inch of her, although he was cautious of what he suspected were her well-defined boundaries. But her skin was warm and his five senses conspired against his good sense until his fingers traveled an inch lower and she suddenly pulled away.

Puzzled, he stared at her, wondering if he'd touched a tender spot, but as he glanced at the point where his hand had roamed on her sternum, he mentally kicked himself for his insensitivity. Clearly, she thought he intended to stray deeper into what she considered forbidden territory.

"I should go to bed," she said, her voice breathy as if she'd been jogging for a mile. "Goodnight."

"Goodnight," he answered to her back as she fled. His night, however, couldn't end with him in his current state. He'd work off his tension in Ty's basement weight room and if that didn't resolve his problem, a cold shower would come next.

All because of the sixty seconds she'd spent in his arms.

Christy spent the next twenty-four hours scolding herself for overreacting to Linc's touch. His gentle caresses hadn't been inappropriate and yet she'd jumped like a frightened virgin.

The truth was she'd enjoyed being in his arms far more than she'd dreamed possible. He was solid and warm and comforting, which gave her such a deep sense of safety—almost as if she was being protected from the latest of life's impending storms. More than that, though, he reminded her of a steady rock she could lean on whenever the need arose.

In spite of all that, she'd jumped away from him like a startled rabbit, she thought with disgust.

She might have apologized, but she didn't see him at all on Monday, although she knew he had come home because he'd left a glass in the sink and a scribbled note on the counter, asking her to pick up his clothes at the dry cleaner's. *Please*, he'd underlined in thick, bold strokes.

On Tuesday, she saw him at the hospital, but

other than a quick "How are the kids?" their conversation had been limited to the status of his patients.

She didn't see him at all on Wednesday, but once again she'd found a note. This time he'd stated how much he'd liked the oatmeal cookies she'd left for him. She'd seen his distinctive scrawl before and thought nothing of it, but his personal message—his compliment—brightened her day. Because she was off duty and intended to spend her hours on household chores and laundry, she needed that bright spot.

Since the kids were in school, she vowed to tackle household projects. She cleaned furiously, debating for the longest time if she should go into Linc's room in case he'd think she was invading his privacy. Finally, after she'd cleaned bedrooms and the community bathroom, she caved in to her own arguments. The man hardly had time to breathe, so he certainly wasn't going to spend his free hours dusting and scrubbing the tub. As neat as he was, he wouldn't notice she'd been in his domain, anyway.

She, however, certainly did. The masculine scent of his bath soap hovered in the bathroom and clung to his towels. Even his bed sheets retained his personal fragrance.

He left more than his scent behind, though. She found other clues that fit the man she knew him to be. The unmade bed suggested he'd been called out early, but even the rumpled bedding testified to Linc's control. A faint indentation of his head on the pillow and one corner of the sheet pulled out from under the mattress hinted that he wasn't a restless sleeper—probably because when he finally closed his eyes, he was too exhausted to move.

Idly, she wondered what he'd be like to sleep with. Would he snuggle up close, like Ria did when it was cold outside, or stick to his side of the bed? Would he pull her toward him or move to the center to meet her?

As she caught herself in her own daydream, she chuckled with embarrassment and was grateful that he wouldn't walk in and discover her locked within her own wicked imagination.

She stripped the bed, forcing a clinical detachment to complete the job.

His full laundry hamper presented another problem. It seemed a horrible waste of water to ask him to launder his things separately—again, when would he even have time?—so she gathered his washables and added them to her other loads, all the while trying not to notice how wifely it felt for his T-shirts and unmentionables to mingle with her own.

Determined to keep her thoughts occupied, she dusted and scrubbed and vacuumed until Ria fled the house for the quiet safety of the back yard. She left nothing unturned, and had even gone into Ty's basement weight room where she'd found a few dirty towels. By the time Emma and Derek were out of school, the place was spotless and she was literally exhausted.

They strolled to the park to exercise Ria and came home at dinnertime, but once again Linc didn't put in an appearance. She didn't see him until the next day at the hospital and then she was certain it was only because Thursday was his normal scheduled surgery day. One of his patients had just been wheeled to a room after waking up in Recovery and Linc had walked in to talk to the man's wife, wearing his green scrubs.

After they'd dealt with the usual order of patient business, he pulled her aside. "When can you get away for lunch?"

"It's hard to say," she admitted. "We're swamped today."

"Make time."

She was tired enough to bristle at his demand—between keeping up with two busy children, a house, and working a short-staffed twelve-hour shift, she now understood why her working-mother colleagues had fragile tempers by the end of the week—but she had to eat and if she didn't take a break soon, her feet would revolt.

"Maybe by one or so," she began.

"Okay. I'll see you then."

He strode away before she could recover from her surprise. As far as the gossip mill had reported, the man rarely took time for himself between his surgical cases and when he did, he usually ate on the run. Could it be he was finally loosening up and becoming more approachable? She smiled at the thought.

Yet as she watched him pause to talk to a pharmacist, then laugh at whatever she'd said, her self-satisfaction dimmed as an unreasonable combination of curiosity and jealousy flooded over her.

Was this the woman he'd mentioned he'd wanted to get to know? If so, then her plan to convince him to enjoy life's simpler pleasures might drive him into another woman's arms.

It was silly of her to consider the possibility. After all, she didn't have any illusions that she was his type.

But, oh, it was nice to dream...

Linc's work schedule for the week hadn't been that unusual for him, but throughout the day—especially during the evenings—he'd caught himself wondering what Christy and the kids might be doing. Knowing that he was missing out had made him impatient at times and he'd earned a number of startled glances from his staff who obviously wondered what had twisted his surgical gloves into a knot.

Each night as he came home he half hoped Christy would be waiting for him, as she had on that first night. Logically, he knew he was expecting too much. Ten-thirty or eleven was late for someone who went to work at five a.m. Not being accustomed to keeping up with two active children, she probably ended her day as soon as Emma and Derek did.

Illogically, he still hoped.

Whenever he walked into a quiet house, those

hopes deflated, although he was pleased by her gesture of leaving the kitchen light blazing so he wouldn't stumble in the dark in the somewhat unfamiliar surroundings.

While she might not physically make an appearance, he felt her presence in other ways—a plate of food in the refrigerator, a pan of frosted brownies on the stove, clean towels in Ty's weight room. Only one thing could have topped them all—if he'd been able to slip into her bed instead of his.

With great relief, he saw his hectic week finally drawing to a close. He could hardly wait another day to talk to her in person instead of through hastily scribbled notes left on the kitchen counter. Yes, he'd seen her a few times at the hospital, but they'd both been coming and going, so conversation had been limited to medical issues.

Today, though, he'd decided to make a change. Before his last case, he'd shocked his surgery staff when he'd announced a thirty-minute break between patients, but he didn't care that he'd wrecked his own routine. He only knew he couldn't wait until Friday night or Saturday morning to see Christy again, and maybe…steal another kiss.

In fact, he couldn't remember the last time he'd

been this eager to meet someone. His job had meant so much to him that it had consumed his existence until most of the personal side of his life had faded away. He'd become somewhat aware of the situation—his time with his brother's family had pointed out what he was missing—but he hadn't discovered a compelling reason to change the habits he'd formed.

Christy had provided it.

A week ago, he'd believed she wasn't right for him with her daring, impulsive approach to life. Oh, he'd been drawn to her like a hapless bug flew toward light, but, given enough opportunity, he was certain he'd eventually purge her from his system. Now, a mere seven days later, it was the last thing he wanted.

His attitude was odd, really. They'd spent more time apart than together, and yet everything he'd seen, everything he'd heard, and everything he'd done only whetted his appetite for more.

The good news was, "more" hung right around the corner.

He returned to the surgery floor at the appointed hour with five minutes to spare, then waited for her to swap an IV fluid bag that had run low. He chafed at the delay, but he was only minutes away from having her to himself, relatively speaking, so he hid his impatience by accessing several lab reports while he listened for her footsteps.

When she returned breathlessly, as if she'd hurried on his account, her smile was worth the wait.

In the cafeteria, he steered her toward a table for two in the corner near the aquarium. Aware of the curious glances directed toward them, he simply ignored everyone and focused on Christy.

"You look tired," he said without preamble as she poured her low-fat dressing over her chef's salad.

"Is it that obvious?" she asked ruefully.

He shrugged as he dug into his roast beef special. "Only to me. You aren't doing too much, are you?"

"Probably, but that's how it works," she quipped. "To be honest, you're looking a little frayed around the edges, too. You aren't the only one with keen powers of observation."

"Apparently not," he answered dryly, surprised she'd picked up the signals others had overlooked. He immediately wondered what else she'd deduced about him. If she had any idea of how easily she triggered a surge in his testosterone level, she'd probably lock herself in her bedroom and never come out.

"I don't know where I'm busier—here at work or at home with the kids. We haven't had a dull moment."

"I've seen the calendar Gail left for us. Next week will be better."

"I don't see how. Between soccer practice two nights and a Cub Scout meeting—"

"I'll be available to help," he interrupted. "The load won't fall completely on you. I'm sorry it did this week, but it won't happen again."

"Don't apologize. A doctor's life doesn't run on a schedule. If it's any consolation, the kids have missed you."

"I've missed you all, too. How did the internet call go last night? No tears when it was all over?"

"A few, but not many. Emma's having a ball, sending emails. You created a monster when you created her own account and showed her how to send letters. I think she's singlehandedly trying to fill her mom's in-box."

"Maybe we should limit her to one or two a day."

"Keeping her too busy to think about sending a message would be better. Forbidding her to contact Gail will only make her more homesick and she'll dwell more on her parents' absence than she should."

He considered her comment. "You're probably right."

"Don't worry. She'll get past this. We simply need to be patient."

"How did you get to be so wise with kids?"

She tipped her bottle of lemonade and drank deeply. "I learned a lot from watching my brother and sisters interact with their children. How about you?"

"My parents constantly reminded me that as the oldest I had to look out for the younger siblings no matter where we were or what we were doing. I'm afraid I wasn't always tactful," he said wryly.

"Ah, you were the bossy older brother."

"Afraid so. I suppose I had more of a dictatorial style, but I think that came from being left in charge so often. My mom had a fantastic voice and a dream to make it big in the country-music scene, so my dad hauled us all over so she could perform and it was my job to keep the little ones busy. As soon as I turned thirteen, they left the three of us at home."

"What did you do to occupy the time?"

"Board games, cards, whatever. You name it, we played it. If I had a dime for every round of *Chutes and Ladders* or *Sorry*, I'd be a wealthy man," he said wryly. "In any case, our main goal was to be awake when our parents came home."

"Were you successful?"

He shook his head. "No. Joanie would usually conk out around eleven, Ty would fall asleep at midnight, and one was my limit."

"Did they do that often? Leave you home alone?"

"Every Saturday night."

"That must have been tough."

He considered for a moment. "It wasn't as tough as it was frustrating. The little kids needed their attention, not mine. I knew my parents loved us, but at times I resented how easily they left us to chase their own dreams."

And that, he knew, was the main reason why he hadn't been in any rush to look for Mrs Right. Although his job guaranteed there would be times when he'd be gone at night, just as his parents had been, he wanted the mother of his children to be a mother twenty-four seven, not just when it was convenient.

"Regardless of their actions, they must have

done something right," she said softly. "You and Ty both turned into responsible adults."

They had, hadn't they? he thought.

"Your story does explain why you take life so seriously," she remarked. "Didn't you ever do anything just for fun?"

"Sure. I hung out with my buddies on Friday nights after football and basketball games. Band kids had to stick together."

"Marching band?"

"I was quite the trumpet player in my day," he said proudly.

"Can you still play?"

"I doubt it." He grinned. "Fortunately for you, I sold my trumpet so we'll never know. By the way, the house looks great. You've been busy."

"I'm surprised you could see a difference. You haven't been home much."

He couldn't tell if she was peeved by his absence or surprised that he was aware of his surroundings even if he came home during the wee hours. He grinned. "You'd be surprised at what I notice. Speaking of which, I don't expect you to clean my room or do my laundry."

"I'm sure you didn't, but I couldn't very well let

your room turn into a pigsty, could I? Gail would kill me."

"Actually, she'd kill *me*," he said wryly. "Regardless, I don't want you taking on more than you need to. I'll ask my housekeeper to add us to her list and—"

"You'll do no such thing." Her voice was firm. "I'm perfectly capable of performing a few chores."

"It isn't a matter of capabilities." He had to tread lightly because he hated to offend her independent spirit. "It's a matter of having enough hours in the day."

"We'll make time. If everyone pitches in, cleaning won't take long at all. 'Many hands make light work,' my mother always says."

"Yes, but, as far as I'm concerned, paying a housekeeper is money well spent."

"I'm sure it is, but I wouldn't feel right if you footed the bill. We're in this together, remember, and, as far as I'm concerned, it's an unnecessary expense."

Her light tone didn't disguise the steel in her voice. He wanted to continue to argue his point, but his gaze landed on the fraying edge of her scrub top's neckline. Nurses might be paid well these days, but thanks to the associated expenses of her illness he suspected money was still tight.

Although he wanted this to be his contribution to the household, he didn't press the issue. "Okay, we'll do it your way. For now," he tacked on his proviso.

"Fair enough."

"So you know, if I had my choice as to what I'd like you to do—cook or clean—I'd choose cooking. What are the odds of getting another batch of those cookies?"

She laughed, clearly amused by his hopeful tone. "That depends on when Derek is scheduled to provide treats for another soccer game."

"Ah, that explains why I couldn't find any more. You gave them away."

She finished her salad. "I did, but you liked them, did you?"

"The best oatmeal cookies I ever tasted."

"Somehow I never saw you as having a sweet tooth."

"I do, which is why I work out three or four times a week. I'm surprised you haven't heard me in the basement."

"You actually exercise when you get home?" She sounded incredulous.

166 UNLOCKING THE SURGEON'S HEART

"Sometimes," he admitted. "Lifting weights helps me work out the kinks if I've been in surgery all day. Sometimes I'm too keyed up to go to sleep, so pumping iron helps."

"Wow. I usually stare mindlessly at the television when I'm exhausted. I'm impressed you're that...disciplined."

"Impressed enough to make another batch of cookies?"

She giggled. "Okay. I'll let you get lucky this weekend."

If she didn't catch the double entendre of her own words, he certainly did. As he glanced at the aquarium and saw those same fish kissing again, he realized his craving went beyond mere cookies. He wanted another taste of Christy and he wanted it as soon as possible.

Getting that taste wouldn't be easy. Underneath her bubbly personality and a layer of friendliness lurked a skittish woman who'd been hurt by someone she'd trusted.

It would be up to him to prove that he was someone she could trust.

CHAPTER SIX

BY FRIDAY, Christy knew she was in trouble. Dredging up the old memories of Jon had fueled her determination to prove that just because she'd had cancer, she was still capable of doing everything any other woman could do. As a result, she'd pushed herself too hard and was paying the price with her nauseous stomach and the headache behind her eyes. She should have been at home because it was her day off, but someone had called in with a family emergency, so as soon as Christy had sent the kids to school, she'd reported to work.

She would have rather spent the day in bed.

There was one silver lining to this dark cloud— she'd arrived on duty after Linc had already made his rounds, otherwise he would have taken one look at her and with the tell-tale twitch in his cheek to indicate his unhappiness he would have insisted she return home. Naturally, she would have had to disobey his command on principle. She was still her own woman and made her own decisions even if, in this case, he was right.

Fortunately, her supervisor had also arranged for a second-shift nurse to come early, so Christy was able to leave as soon as Derek and Emma's school day ended.

She swallowed several anti-inflammatories and painkillers, and soldiered on through the rest of the afternoon—even making Linc's requested cookies—but by dinner's end her own food refused to stay in her stomach and she finally had to face facts. Her body had reached its limit.

"Are you guys ready for bed?" she asked, hoping she sounded brighter than she felt.

Derek was horrified. "We never go to bed at seven, even on school nights. Fridays is our night to stay up late 'cause Mom wants us to sleep in on Saturdays."

"Yeah," Emma chimed in. "It is."

"Then you do sleep late on Saturdays?" Christy asked, because so far they hadn't.

Derek's grin was sheepish. "Sometimes, but if we don't and Mom or Dad aren't awake, we know not to bother them."

Thank you, Gail, for training them properly, she

thought with some relief. "I'd suggest you snooze as long as you can. We have a full day tomorrow."

Derek was suspicious. "Doing what?"

She had no idea, but surely Linc had a plan. "I have to discuss it with your uncle first," she prevaricated.

"We can watch a movie now, can't we?" Derek asked.

"Yeah." Emma's head bobbed enthusiastically. "Mom lets us on a Friday."

She hated to park them in front of the television, but common sense told her that Gail and Ty allowed them to watch their movies if the size of the children's collection was any indication. As for leaving them alone, she also knew their parents didn't hover over them every second. They were school-aged children, not toddlers who required constant supervision.

"Okay, but after that, it's bedtime."

"Sure." Emma peered at her. "You don't look so good, Christy. Are you sick?"

She managed a smile. "A little. I'm going to lie down, but I want you to get me if you need anything. Anything at all. Is that understood?"

"Sure."

"And don't eat all the cookies. Save some for your uncle."

"We will," the two said in unison.

"Don't forget to wake me in half an hour or when your uncle arrives, whichever comes first."

"We will."

As the opening credits appeared on the screen, Christy dropped onto her bed. Ria padded in and curled against her in her usual, I'm-here-for-you-because-I-know-you-don't-feel-well position.

Christy patted the dog's head in gratitude for her faithfulness before she promptly closed her eyes and tried to relax.

"All I need are thirty minutes," she murmured aloud. "Just thirty minutes and I'll be ready to go. Linc will never know I couldn't keep up. How much trouble can two kids cause while watching a movie, anyway?"

Linc was more than ready to be home. His hospital patients were stable, including the emergency splenectomy case, and, barring a car accident, he should have a quiet evening ahead of him.

He strode into the house at seven forty-five, expecting to see three smiling faces eager to enjoy the remaining daylight. Instead, he walked into a kitchen that resembled a disaster area, with stacks of dirty pots and pans, spilled juice, and a popcorn trail that led into the living room.

Before he could wrap his head around the unusual scene, Emma came running and launched herself into his arms.

"Unca Linc's home!"

"Hi, sprout. How are you?" he asked as he settled her on his hip.

"I'm fine. Christy's sick."

Emma's revelation explained the mess. Immediately, he tried to recall what bug was making the rounds now, and came up blank. "She is? Was she sick all day?"

Emma shrugged. "Just since dinner. She's in bed so you hafta be quiet. Derek and I are watching a movie. We missed you, Unca Linc." She flung her arms around his neck and hugged him.

Not for the first time in his life, Linc was envious of his brother. This was what Ty came home to every night, not an empty house with a radio or television for company.

This, he decided—coming home to a wife and kids and even an occasional mess—was what he wanted, too. Preferably sooner rather than later.

"We missed you."

"I missed you, too." He prodded for information. "What's wrong with Christy?"

"I think it's her stomach because I heard her throwing up. She told us to wake her when you came home. Do you want me to get her?"

"That's okay. I'll check on her myself," he told her as he lowered her until her feet touched the floor.

"Christy left a plate for you in the 'frigerator," Emma offered helpfully, before she headed for the living room. "I'm gonna watch the rest of our movie."

Whatever Christy had served definitely smelled delicious and from the looks of the pots and pans on the stove, she'd served spaghetti. Although he wanted to dig into his own serving, he chose to wait until he discovered what was wrong with Christy.

He strolled through the living room, past the two children, who were engrossed in their movie, and stopped at Christy's door. When she didn't answer his knock, he peeked inside and saw her lying in bed with a watchful Ria at her side.

"Christy?" he asked softly.

She stirred. "Linc?"

"It's me," he assured her. "I hear you're not feeling well."

"I'm okay. Dinner's in—"

"The refrigerator. Emma told me." He strode in and stood next to her bed, worried that whatever had hit her had laid her so low and so quickly.

"I still need to clean the kitchen." She grimaced as she tried to rise.

"The kitchen can wait. Do I need to phone your doctor? Call in a prescription?" He imagined all sorts of possible causes and treatments—some dire, some run-of-the-mill—as he gently placed his hand on her forehead. Her skin felt cool, which eased his worries to some degree.

"No. Please, no. It's nothing."

He disagreed. "What's wrong? Stomach flu?" He'd already ruled out a chest cold because she breathed easily and her nose wasn't running.

"No, just overtired."

"Overtired?" His momentary panic eased. "I thought you agreed to pace yourself."

"I know, and I tried, but I felt so wonderful and thought I could do it all, so I did. Unfortunately, pushing my limits caught up to me today." She met his gaze for an instant before she closed her eyes. "I know you want to, so go ahead and scold."

She sounded defeated as well as sick, so he opted for mercy. "I'll wait until you're feeling better," he teased. "It's tough to kick a man—or woman—when she's already down."

"Thanks. Just give me another hour or so. I'll feel better by then. Honest."

Linc doubted it. Her face was too pale and the circles under her eyes too dark for him to believe a mere hour's nap would solve her problems, but he didn't intend to argue with her.

"Okay," he said evenly. "Can I get you something in the meantime? Hot tea? Aspirin?"

"I'm fine, thanks, although I'd appreciate it if you could let Ria outdoors. She hasn't had a bathroom break for a while."

"Will do." He snapped his fingers. "Come, Ria. Outside?"

Ria perked her ears as if she wanted to obey, but from the way she glanced at Christy, then back at him, she was torn between obeying nature's call and comforting her mistress.

"Come on, girl," he coaxed. "Take care of business and you can join Christy again."

Reluctantly, Ria rose, stretched, then gracefully leaped off the bed. Linc opened the patio door and as soon as Ria returned from a trip to her favorite bush, she ignored the tasty popcorn trail and disappeared into Christy's bedroom.

Certain the animal was now cuddled against her owner, Linc had one thought as he microwaved his dinner.

He was jealous of a dog.

After he'd eaten, washed the dishes, changed into a pair of comfortable gym shorts and an old T-shirt, he carried in a cup of tea prepared the way she liked it—with one teaspoon of honey—and stayed with her until she drank it.

He spent the rest of the evening watching movies, playing a few hands of *Go Fish* and *Old Maid* with Derek and Emma, and checking on Christy.

"I'm going to float away," she grumbled as he helped her sit so she could drink another cup of tea.

"Better that than getting dehydrated," he said cheerfully. As soon as she'd emptied most of the cup and lay down again, he returned to the living room and found both children fighting to stay awake.

For the next hour he oversaw their bedtime ritual and read the obligatory two stories, with an extra book for good measure.

"Christy said we had big plans for tomorrow,"

Derek mentioned as he crawled between the sheets. "What are we doing?"

Linc thought fast. "We'll see how she feels," he hedged, "but I thought we could spend the day at my house. My weeds are probably knee-high by now."

"Can I ride the mower with you?" Derek asked, his tired eyes brimming with excitement.

"Maybe," he said. "Now go to sleep and we'll talk about it in the morning."

Outside Christy's room, he paused in indecision, but a noise in the kitchen drew him there instead. He found Christy leaning against the counter, a cupboard door open, as if she'd been trying to retrieve a glass but hadn't quite managed it.

"How are you feeling?" he asked.

She straightened with obvious effort. "Better. I came to wash the dishes, but everything's done."

Because she sounded almost irritated, he fought back a smile. "It gave me something to do while the kids finished their movie."

"Where are they?"

"In bed, ready to wake up at the crack of dawn for a fun-filled, action-packed day at the Maguire house." He motioned to the cupboard. "Can I get you something?"

"Water, please."

He filled a glass and placed it beside her.

"You should have left the dishes for me," she said in between sips. "I said I'd—"

"Yes, I know, but I didn't mind," he said calmly. "There weren't that many, so it didn't take long. I didn't even get dishpan hands. See?" He held up his hands to show her.

To his surprise, then dismay, a few tears trickled down her face and she swiped them away with her fingertips. Oh, man. She was *crying*.

"Hey," he protested. "Washing a few pots and pans isn't anything to get upset over."

"I'm not." She sniffed.

From where he was standing, she certainly seemed as if she was. "If you're not upset," he said carefully, "then what's wrong?"

"I'd wanted everything to be perfect when you finally came home."

"It was," he assured her. At her skeptical glance, he corrected himself. "Maybe not *perfect*, but it was close."

"No, it wasn't."

"Hey, the kids were fed and my dinner was

waiting for me. Having only a few dirty dishes waiting was pretty darned good, in my opinion."

"That's not the point. I—"

"If you were afraid I'd find fault, I apologize. You don't have to impress me, Christy, because I've been impressed since our first weekend."

She met his gaze, her smile wan. "How could you be?"

"Trust me. I am."

Her expression revealed her skepticism. "I truly wanted to amaze you with what I could do and how well I could keep up, but I'd really wanted to convince myself." She raked her hair with one hand. "And I failed."

She'd caught him off guard. "You wanted to impress yourself? Why?"

"After thinking about Jon the other night, I realized that all this time I've been trying to prove him wrong—that my cancer treatments wouldn't make me less of a woman than any other. That I could still juggle the same things every other woman juggles in her life, even if I lacked a few body parts and didn't have the same hormones swimming around my system. He'd never know if I'd succeeded or not, but *I* would know the truth."

She paused and her shoulders drooped. "I'm beginning to think he was right."

Furious with Jon's insensitivity and angry at himself for dredging up enough of the past to rob her of her confidence, he held her by her shoulders. "Absolutely do *not* mention or think about that man's narrow-mindedness again. You've done a remarkable job when it comes to balancing work and children and a house. Do not *ever* suggest or even *think* otherwise. Got that?" he ground out.

She blinked several times before she nibbled on her bottom lip.

He squeezed her shoulders and gave her a slight shake. "Did you hear what I said?"

"I heard. But—"

He gentled his hold as well as his voice. "You have nothing to prove to me or to anyone else, and I don't want you to try." He nudged her chin upward with his index finger so her gaze could meet his. "You're tired and aren't feeling well, so it's easy to let your imagination and your fears run wild, but, honestly, no one in this house has any reason to complain about what you have or haven't done, least of all me. I'm the one who's been absent without leave for the past five days."

She hesitated, her face pensive as if she was

giving his words some thought. "So you're saying I should complain about you?"

"If it'll make you feel better, yes."

Her chuckle was weak but, nonetheless, it was still a chuckle. "I'll pass."

"Good, because I'm not sure my fragile ego could take it. For the record, there's no shame in recognizing one's limitations and delegating accordingly. If we could manage everything ourselves, we wouldn't need each other, would we?"

Her downcast expression suddenly turned thoughtful. "I suppose not."

"Good. Now, finish your water and hop into bed where you belong. Tomorrow will roll around soon enough and I have a few plans on how we'll spend the day."

She nodded, but didn't move. Instead, her gaze continued to rest on him until he felt almost uncomfortable.

"Do I have spaghetti sauce on my chin?" he joked.

"No, but this is the first time I think I've ever seen you so passionate about something. Normally, you're so...so *controlled*."

"People respond better if their surgeon is controlled and doesn't rant and rave like a lunatic when he's aggravated," he said lightly.

"You can be passionate without being out of control. Watching you express your emotion is... comforting, I guess. You seem so much more... *natural*. I like seeing you less formal."

He could think of many other ways to show her just how passionate he could be, but now wasn't the time and the kitchen wasn't the place. It was, however, reassuring to realize he didn't have to hide his innermost feelings around her. He could relax and be himself, such as he was.

"You'll see my emotional side more often in the coming weeks after we all start to get on each other's nerves," he said in a dry tone. "In the meantime, you need your rest."

"I'm tired but I'm not sleepy. Does that make sense?"

"It makes perfect sense," he said as he led her toward her room, "but I'll tell you what I tell the kids. Get ready for bed and by the time you're finished, you'll change your mind."

He turned down her sheets while she slipped into the bathroom, then returned to the living room where he sprawled on the sofa and debated if he needed another trip to Ty's weight room before he called it a day, too.

However, when she appeared wearing her sleepshirt that hit her midthigh, every part of his body seemed to notice just how long her legs were. "Do you need anything?" he asked her, hoping his voice didn't sound as hoarse as it did to his own ears.

"Stay with me," she said.

He froze, certain his hearing had suddenly and inexplicably failed. "Stay?" he echoed as surprise paralyzed his lungs for a few seconds.

"Talk to me until I fall asleep," she said. "Please?"

He simply rose and followed her like a lemming. He couldn't explain why he obeyed—perhaps it was the plea in her voice and on her face. Perhaps he was just a glutton for punishment. Whatever the reason, he knew he couldn't refuse.

As he watched the slight sway of her trim hips, he decided that he deserved a sainthood for what he was about to do. His discomfort increased as she crawled into bed with her nightshirt riding dangerously high over her delightful backside, and he hardly noticed Ria standing at the foot of the bed, watching what her humans would do next.

The instant Christy scooted across the full-sized bed that was hardly large enough for her and patted the spot beside her, he immediately lost his ability to breathe or swallow. He'd expected to sit beside the bed, not share it.

"Please?" she asked.

Considering how she'd nearly jumped out of her skin when he'd touched her the other day, her request seemed out of character. Only able to arrive at one reason for her change of heart, he narrowed his eyes to study her with a physician's objectivity. Her pupils appeared normal, but he still had to wonder if she was acting under the effects of a drug or suffering from some sort of chemical reaction.

"What have you taken?" he asked, suspicious.

"Over-the-counter stuff," she said. "Why?"

Telling her that he thought she was high on drugs wouldn't win him any brownie points.

"No reason," he said, resigned to a very long workout after she'd dozed off.

"I know I'm asking a lot of you but, as comforting as Ria is, our conversations are one-sided. If you don't want to, though…"

He wanted to, and if she knew how badly he wanted it, she'd have locked her door before he'd come inside. However, he must have paused too long to answer because she suddenly sat up and wrapped her arms around her knees in a protective gesture.

"Forget it," she said. "I shouldn't have asked. I knew better, but I'd hoped you were comfortable enough…"

Once again, he mentally kicked himself. She'd seen his hesitation as a sign of distaste when in reality he was simply trying to keep his body under control.

"Trust me, I want to be here, beside you," he said as he lowered his weight onto the bed. "If you knew how much, though, you'd rethink your request."

Idly, he noticed Ria had disappeared but the telltale sound of her scratching her pallet as if making her nest told him the animal had accepted his place in Christy's bed.

Christy hadn't responded. Thinking she might be reconsidering her request, he glanced at her and saw her eyes wide with disbelief. "Really?" She hesitated, her teeth worrying her lower lip,

"You're not just saying that because you feel sorry—"

"Sweetheart, right now I'm feeling a lot of things and 'sorry' isn't on that list." He held out his left arm as an open invitation and she slowly curled against him.

It was heaven. It was hell. He persevered as she wriggled to find a comfortable position with her head resting on his shoulder and her body plastered against his. He inhaled sharply, but that, too, was a mistake because her sweet scent filled his nostrils.

Hoping conversation would focus his attention on subjects other than her physical presence and how great she felt in his arms, he asked, "What should we talk about?"

"I don't care. Whatever you like."

He wanted to point out that she was the one who'd requested conversation, but didn't. He simply had to think of this as being similar to sitting beside Derek or Emma as he read or told bedtime stories.

Unfortunately, the circumstances weren't the same; they didn't compare in any way, shape, or form.

"Okay," he said, casting about for a place to

start. "Do you always get physically ill when you're overtired?"

"No. I wasn't like this B.C., before chemo. I keep hoping it'll fade, but it hasn't. Normally, I do a better job of pacing myself, but taking care of Derek and Emma is like a dream come true. I was like the Energizer Bunny. I kept going and going and going."

"Why? You have two months to fill Gail's shoes."

"Two months in which to pack a lifetime of mothering," she corrected. "If I never have kids of my own, I have to store up the memories when I borrow someone else's."

"You don't know that you won't ever be a mother."

"I also don't know if I will."

"No one has guarantees," he pointed out. "I hate to break it to you, but you're like the rest of us. Fertility for anyone isn't a given. If it were, there wouldn't be specialty clinics all over the country."

"Hmm. I never thought of it like that. But you have to admit the odds of my hormones staying on a permanent sabbatical are much greater."

"People beat the odds every day. However, if you don't..." he shrugged "...there are a host of other ways to have a family. Your real problem is that you worry too much."

She snickered. "I do, don't I? So tell me, why don't you let anyone see your emotions and the passion inside you?"

It took him a minute to follow her conversation shift because she'd started rubbing her fingers against his heart and the contact was doing crazy things to his nerve endings. He placed his hand over hers to stop the gentle torment as he spoke.

"People trust me with their lives. They want to feel confident about the person who's cutting them open and messing around with their insides. Patients prefer a surgeon who is cool, calm, and collected under fire, not one whose emotions are constantly on display."

"I suppose you're right." She burrowed deeper against him and sighed like a contented kitten, which effectively sent a fresh surge of blood into his groin.

"I know I am."

Her words came slower, which made him think she was finally starting to doze. A few seconds later, she spoke again.

"Why aren't you married by now?"

"I haven't found the right woman," he answered.

"Have you been looking?"

"Not seriously," he admitted.

"Why not?"

There was something about the darkness that made it easier to share things he only admitted to himself. "I had this idea to wait until I was forty."

"Forty? Gracious. Your life will be half-over."

He grinned at her affronted tone. For a woman who wrung every minute of joy from her day, he was surprised she had such a glass-half-empty attitude. Then again, if he'd endured what she had, aware that any day could be his last, hindsight would paint those years as wasted, too. As he'd already pointed out, life didn't come with guarantees.

Unsettled by his epiphany, he went on to explain. "I suppose I wanted my future spouse to be settled in her career like I was, wanting the same things I did when it came to raising a family. I'd met a few women who'd interested me, but there always seemed to be something missing."

"No passion?"

Was that it? Possibly. Probably. Whatever the reason, he'd never felt compelled to pursue them. Christy, however, was the exception.

"What about the lady you told me about?"

"Which lady?"

"You know. The one you said you wanted to get to know."

He had to think a minute to remember…and when he did, he was grateful the room was too dark for her to see his grin. "Oh, *that* woman."

"So, Romeo, are you going to ask her out?" Her body tensed, as if bracing herself for his answer.

"Definitely."

Because it was dark, he sensed rather than saw her disappointment. "That's nice," she answered, although her words lacked sincerity.

He wanted to believe she was jealous; he certainly hoped so because it meant she had feelings for him. His for her were certainly multiplying at an exponential rate.

"What's she like? Is she pretty?"

"I think she's beautiful, but I get the impression she wouldn't agree."

"What attracted you to her? I'll bet she has a great body. Doesn't have a single scar either."

Once again, he heard her mournful tone. "She has scars, but I'm a surgeon so they don't bother me. I think of them as badges of courage."

"Oh, what a great description. What else can you tell me about her?"

"She's sweet." As she snorted at that remark, he continued, "And kind. She'd do anything for her friends. She loves kids and is definitely a dog person."

She sighed. "She sounds perfect."

"Oh, she has her flaws, but to me no one else compares."

"Where will you take her on your first date?"

"I haven't decided yet. Where would you suggest?"

"My choice would be Grant's Point," she said, her voice growing softer. "It's a very peaceful, romantic spot. You can reach out and touch the stars while you hear the wind whisper through the trees and smell the pines. There's no place better."

If memory served him, the landmark was a famous place for couples to visit. Local folklore suggested the majority of Levitt Springs' population had been conceived on that overlook. Regardless, if the hill was Christy's choice, he'd take her there.

However, she seemed to be speaking from experience and he hated the idea of another guy taking her there, even if only for a platonic let's-see-the-local-hot-spots trip.

"You've been there before?"

"Ria and I drove there one night and watched the stars come out. It was great. You and your lady friend will enjoy it."

He was uncommonly pleased to hear Ria had been her date. "I'm positive we will."

"If you want, she can take my place as your dance partner." Her reluctance was evident, as if she didn't want to extend the offer but good manners demanded it.

"I'm happy with the partner I have."

"If you change your mind…"

"I won't," he assured her.

"Thank you."

He wondered what she was thanking him for—for not changing his mind or for being happy to have her as his partner. Maybe it was simply because he wasn't rejecting her in favor of another woman.

For a long minute he only heard her gentle breathing and he thought she'd finally fallen asleep, but before he could move a muscle, she spoke again.

"I'm sorry for jumping out of my skin the other night when you touched me." She slurred her words and he wondered if she realized she was speaking.

"It's okay. I understand."

"It's not okay. I wanted you to do what you did, but—"

"But what?"

"I don't feel anything," she said flatly. "Men expect a woman to respond, but I can't because they aren't feeling *me*. If you don't mind, I need your help."

Clinically he understood her dilemma, but personally he sensed a minefield had appeared in front of him. He could only hope she wouldn't remember this conversation in the morning. "Help with what?"

"Help me so I don't jump next time," she said. "We could practice."

He swallowed hard. "Practice?"

Her nod felt as if she was nuzzling his shoulder with her nose. "That way, if I ever meet a fellow and he—"

The idea that she wanted him to condition her to handle another man's touch nearly made him growl with frustration. As uninhibited as her exhaustion had made her, if she'd asked to begin now, *he* would be the one jumping out of his skin, not to mention her bed. Although he was male enough to be grateful she had asked *him* for help.

"Sorry, but that isn't something we should do. You'll have to wing it when the time comes."

Once again, she sighed. "You're right. Your girl-friend wouldn't understand, would she?"

For lack of anything else to say, he resorted to, "No, she wouldn't."

"You know something?" She slurred her words. "I was prepared to dislike you, but you're a very nice man."

He grinned like a loon. "I'm glad you think so."

"It's too bad, though."

"Oh?" he asked.

"Because it wouldn't take much for me to fall in love."

His breath froze in his lungs. "Would that be so terrible?" he asked softly.

"Not terrible," she murmured. "It would be wonderful. Not a good idea, though."

"Why not?" he asked.

One minute of silence stretched into two, then into five, but she didn't answer. He wanted to nudge her awake so she could reply to his question, but he was reasonably certain she wouldn't remember what she'd said.

He, however, wouldn't forget.

Another five minutes went by. With great regret, Linc eased out from under her, covered her bare legs with a sheet, then tiptoed from the room.

He'd never imagined the evening would end with the two of them engaging in pillow talk. If another woman had said she could fall in love with him, he would have run for the nearest exit, but hearing Christy admit those feelings only reinforced his determination to hold on to her in any way he could.

Aware of his lingering arousal, he headed once again to the basement. At the rate he was going, he'd develop a bodybuilder's physique before Ty and Gail returned.

CHAPTER SEVEN

"I THINK Jose is well enough to go home, don't you?" Linc said to Christy after he'd reviewed Jose's chart five days later.

"He's doing remarkably well," she agreed. "He's complaining about the food again, so he's definitely feeling better." Between the filter that had been surgically inserted and medication adjustments, his most recent tests showed the clot in his leg was nearly dissolved.

Linc clicked a few final computer keys before he logged off the terminal. "I'll break the news to him while you get things rolling."

"Will do."

He scooted his chair away from the counter. "You have a sitter for tonight, right?"

"Heather's coming over at seven," she told him. Heather was the sixteen-year-old high-school girl who came early on the mornings Christy had to work and oversaw Derek and Emma getting ready for school. Sometimes Linc was still there, but more often than not he'd left early, too, so Heather's presence was a godsend.

"Although I still don't understand why we need a sitter while we practice a dance routine," she grumbled good-naturedly. "Derek and Emma won't bother us."

He raised an eyebrow. "If they don't, it would be a first," he said wryly.

"I agree they're rather clingy, but they're still adjusting."

"I understand that, but even if by some miracle they would give us an hour to ourselves, I'd rather not risk it. Constant interruptions aren't conducive to learning what we need to learn. The competition is only six weeks away."

As if she needed reminding. She'd fielded more questions about being Linc's partner, and from some of the comments she'd overheard, most were surprised to hear of his participation. Speculation and curiosity had increased ticket sales, as she'd suspected would happen. She only hoped Linc hadn't heard those same rumors because, knowing his determination to excel, he'd insist on incorporating a more advanced routine than necessary.

"Regardless, everything is set for tonight," she said.

"Great." With that, he rose and headed to Jose's room.

Less than a minute later, one of the other nurses, Rose Warren, strode into the nurses' station, looking over her shoulder with eyes wide and her jaw slack.

"I can't believe it," she remarked to Christy. "Did you see him?"

"See who?" Christy answered as she pulled the appropriate discharge forms and patient home-care instructions from various folders.

"Dr Maguire." Rose stared in the direction she'd come. "The man *smiled* at me."

Christy grinned. "How absolutely terrible."

"I wonder what's happened? I mean, he's always been courteous but he's never gone out of his way to be friendly."

"Yes, he has," she protested mildly.

"To you, maybe. To the rest of us, he's just... *polite*."

Was Rose right? Christy thought for a moment and suspected there was some truth to her observation, but if Linc spoke to her more often than anyone else, it was only because most of the staff didn't bother including him in their conversations. Granted, they'd probably tried at one point and his usual monosyllabic answers had eventually convinced them to stop trying, but she'd been undaunted. She'd always forced him into a discussion that didn't involve treatment plans or patient symptoms and over the two years she'd known him they'd progressed to single sentences. Now, though, he didn't wait to speak until spoken to, which was quite an achievement, in her opinion.

"He's a very quiet, reserved person," she countered, "but once you get to know him, he's a great guy."

"Well, whatever you're doing to put the smile on his face, keep it up."

She wasn't doing anything in particular, although she had to admit that ever since Linc had sat with her while she'd fallen asleep, she'd caught him staring at her with the most amazing twinkle in his eyes. She must have said something amusing, but she couldn't remember what it must have been. She recalled asking him why he hadn't married, as well as a host of other questions regarding the woman he wanted to get to know. In a fuzzy corner in her memory she thought she'd apologized for jumping out of her skin when he'd touched her, and had told him why, but the rest was a blur between reality and a dream.

However, when she pressed him for details, he simply smiled, which made her wonder if she'd talked in her sleep.

It was probably best if she didn't know what she'd said while her defenses had been down because she'd never be able to face him again.

"I wonder if he's seeing someone," Rose said thoughtfully.

The idea gave her a moment's pause, but unless he carved out time in his already busy days, she couldn't conceive how it might be possible. Although she wasn't trying to keep him from his lady friend, she was, however, pleased that he'd devoted his evenings to her and the children.

"Could be," she said in a noncommittal tone.

Rose's dark eyes grew speculative. "Aren't the two of you looking after his brother's family while they're out of the country?"

"Yes."

"How's that working out?"

Christy was nothing if not circumspect. "Fine. You know how it is with kids, there's hardly time to breathe."

Once again, Rose glanced in the direction he'd

disappeared. "If a love interest hasn't lightened his mood, then being around you must have done the trick."

Linc *had* spent far more time at home than she'd initially expected. While he still had definite ideas about how and when things should be done, he'd also been more willing to compromise than she'd dreamed possible.

"Unless..." Rose stared at Christy thoughtfully "...you two are having a romance."

Christy fought the warmth spreading up her neck and into her face. "Don't be ridiculous. He's just getting into the spirit of the hospital fundraiser," she prevaricated. "Have you bought your tickets yet?"

"I have. Dean and I are looking forward to a night out." She grinned. "Even if we have to spend it with the same people we work with."

"Oh, the sacrifices one must make."

"Where are you going on your vacation this year?" Rose asked. "Let me guess. You're running the bulls."

Christy laughed. "Sorry, that's in July and I've missed it for this year."

"Maybe you can do one of those Ironman events."

"I'm not in shape for it."

"You're not in shape for what?" Linc's voice interrupted.

"An Ironman event," Christy explained. "You know—those endurance events that involve swimming, biking, and a marathon run."

"We were discussing ideas for her annual adventure," Rose added helpfully. "She's already missed running with the bulls, but I suppose she could always do something wild like climbing Mount Everest."

"Sorry," Christy answered cheerfully, noting how Linc had suddenly tensed. "Too cold."

Rose turned to Linc. "Do you have any suggestions for her, Doctor?"

A predatory gleam appeared in his eyes as he met Christy's gaze and the heat she saw caused all her nerve endings to tingle.

"Not off the top of my head," he said. "But I'll give the subject some thought."

Hearing that Christy was looking for a new adventure activated a fiercely protective streak he hadn't noticed before. He didn't want her choosing a dangerous pastime and he certainly didn't want her getting her thrills in the company of some other guy, no matter how innocent the circumstances might be.

As for suggesting an exciting activity, he had an idea and it had driven him to the weight bench on several occasions. It involved the two of them, alone on a deserted island and surrounded only by the sun, sand, and the sea. Unfortunately, the rest of his mental picture wasn't suitable to mention to a relative stranger and he was certain Christy wasn't ready to hear it either.

Some things a man had to keep to himself until the proper moment.

However, he'd planned an adventure of another sort for this very evening—Christy didn't know about it, yet—and he spent most of his afternoon keeping close tabs on the clock. If his office staff thought he was unusually eager to leave, they were too polite to comment.

At six forty-five, after promising Derek and Emma that he'd make up for missing their bedtime story, Linc promptly ushered Christy into his car. Tonight was their first private dance lesson and he couldn't decide if he was dreading the experience or looking forward to it. He hoped the instructor would be as good as his billing because he didn't want to disappoint Christy with his two left feet.

He passed the street leading to her apartment, then turned in the opposite direction from his house when she spoke.

"Linc," she said carefully, "I thought we were going to practice a dance routine."

"We are."

"Then where are we going?"

He made a right turn. "I've scheduled private lessons for us at the You Can Dance studio."

Her jaw visibly dropped. "However did you manage that? They're booked for weeks in advance and that's just for a *group* lesson. I can't imagine what one would have to do for a private session."

"Yeah, well." He shrugged. "It's who you know. In my case, one of my patients is a relative and he put in a good word for me."

"I should be angry with you," she said without heat. "First you announce at dinner that your housekeeper will come by every week and now you've arranged for private dance lessons? What's next? A caterer?"

He chuckled at her obvious frustration. "Catering is definitely out, but we have a dance routine to perfect," he reminded her, "and that won't happen overnight. So, to be sure we have time to devote, it only makes sense for Paullina to take on a few of our housekeeping chores. It isn't a reflection on you, I swear."

She fell silent and he hoped she was weighing the benefits and not preparing to present new arguments. "Okay," she conceded, "but the minute we don't need her—"

Gail and Ty would be home. However, he didn't want to mention, or think about, the day when their familial interlude would end. In the meantime, whether he turned into an overnight dance sensation or not, he intended to practice his steps with Christy as often as possible until he had another legitimate reason—one she would accept—to hold her in his arms.

"She'll be gone. I promise." He parked in a space in front of the studio's entrance. "Shall we see what Mario and Carmen can do for us?"

Mario and Carmen were a Cuban husband-and-wife team in their mid-thirties and they greeted them with wide smiles.

"What would you like to dance for your competition?" Mario asked in his distinctive Spanish accent.

Linc shared a glance with Christy. "We're open to suggestions."

"Then we will show you various types of dance and you can choose which one speaks to you."

As the couple demonstrated everything from the tango to mambo, the Viennese waltz to a foxtrot, with a fluidity that Linc envied, he began to wonder what he'd gotten himself into. Christy obviously sensed his concern, because she'd threaded her arm through his in a most comforting manner.

Halfway through the session, Carmen started the music for "The Time of My Life". As he watched the pair perform the steps Patrick Swayze had made famous, he knew what he wanted. The sparkle in Christy's eyes and her tight grip on his arm suggested she agreed.

"A good choice," Mario said when Linc announced their decision. "I'm afraid some of the steps might be too much for you to learn in such a short time. The lift, for instance."

"Then modify it for us," Linc said, "because that, or something similar, is what we want."

Mario grinned. "Ah, I like to see determination. That is good because you must work hard. We will meet only twice a week, but you will practice every day."

Linc had anticipated the order and was looking forward to it. "We will."

The lessons began. Ten minutes into the session, Mario pulled him aside.

"You are trying too hard, *amigo*. You wish to impress the lady, no?"

Frustrated by his missteps that made it difficult for Christy to follow, Linc rubbed his face with both hands. "Am I that obvious?"

"Only to me," Mario assured him. "Don't think about what you're feet are doing. This is a song of love between you and your partner and has nothing to do with people out there." He swept out his arm toward an imaginary audience. "As you express your feelings, you will relax and move with the confidence of a man who has a prize that many others want but cannot have."

He recognized the truth in his instructor's comments, but he hadn't earned the prize either.

Mario must have seen something on Linc's face because he smiled. "Ah, so that's how it is. You are not certain you've won."

Linc shrugged sheepishly. "No."

"But you are here and they are not, so that gives you an advantage, does it not?" He paused. "She is a beautiful woman."

Linc didn't hesitate. "She is."

Mario winked. "And do you not think so many men will be envious of you?"

He grinned. "Probably."

"Then be confident that for this moment she is yours and only yours. When you move securely in that knowledge, your feet will go where they need to and she will follow."

Yours and only yours.

He liked the sound of that. Furthermore, he suddenly realized that he wanted far more than only a moment. He didn't know how or when it had happened, but he wanted weeks, months, and *years* with her. He also wanted the clock to begin now, not later after her check-up.

"Shall we try again?" Mario asked.

He drew a bracing breath. "Okay. Let's do this."

The instructor clapped his hands. "Good. Then we begin."

By the end of the session Linc was exhausted and he was certain Christy's head was spinning from all the turns they'd practiced, but as soon as he'd put Mario's advice into play, he'd felt himself become more sure-footed.

Mario pulled him aside as they were leaving. "Well done. I can see your confidence growing, no? Perhaps when you return you will be the teacher and I will be the student?"

Linc laughed. "I appreciate the thought, but that would take a miracle."

Mario smiled, his teeth white in his tanned face. "Stranger things have happened, no? Now, go home and practice. We will see your progress at the next session."

"Linc," Christy cried three nights later as she collapsed on the sofa after another set of spins. "No more. Please."

Linc grinned. "You aren't wimping out on me now, are you? What happened to the woman who's looking for an adventure?"

"She's tired and if she turns one more time, she's going to do something horrible, like deposit her dinner on your feet." She rubbed her midsection in an effort to calm her stomach.

He sank onto the cushions beside her. "Poor baby. I have been working you hard, haven't I?"

"To put it mildly. You haven't forgotten this is just a friendly competition, have you?"

"No, but anything worth doing…"

"Is worth doing well." She finished his saying because if she'd heard it once, she'd heard it a hundred times. "Now I understand how you became such a brilliant surgeon. You give new meaning to the word 'single-minded.'"

"Thanks. I think."

"You're welcome. The good news is that Mario and Carmen should be pleased when we see them tomorrow night."

"They certainly should be," he said, sounding pleased with himself. "We're positively awesome."

She had to admit, they were. Of course, Mario and Carmen had only assigned them a few steps to perfect, but they had learned those well. While she'd always had a good sense of rhythm, Linc had completely surprised her. He moved so naturally to the music, she couldn't believe she'd ever thought him stilted and straitlaced.

"You never did say why Mario pulled you aside," she said, curious.

"He gave me a pep talk. He said I was trying too hard."

"You were." She'd seen him struggling and she'd found his determination endearing. She'd also been tempted to suggest they try something less complicated, but Carmen had stopped her.

"Men are simple creatures," she'd said. *"They*

give gifts to the ones they care about. He wants to do this for you, so you must not deny him the chance."

Now, three days later, the notion that he might care about her made her smile with delight. On the other hand, when she wasn't reveling in those female feelings, she was having a panic attack. She didn't want to fall in love with him, even though she feared she'd already marched halfway down that path.

Besides, Carmen must have misread Linc's signals because someone else had already captured his eye. If Linc seemed determined to master this particular dance, proving that he could was his only motivation.

She pinched her thumb and forefinger together. "By then, I was this close to suggesting we stick to a simple waltz."

"Won't happen," he said firmly. "I'd already made up my mind."

Once he'd reached a decision, she knew nothing short of an act of God would convince him to change his mind. "What exactly did Mario say to get you to relax?"

"That I'd be the envy of every man watching,

so I might as well enjoy myself. Those weren't his exact words, but they're close."

Certainly the women in the audience would feel the same about her, she thought. It was inevitable as she would have the most handsome man in the hospital at her side.

"By the end of the evening, you'll be on every single woman's radar," she said lightly.

"Won't matter," he said firmly. "There's only one on mine."

She ignored the instant pain she felt. "When *are* you going to ask out this paragon of virtue?"

"Soon."

"How soon?"

"You seem awfully concerned about my dating habits."

"Only because I don't want to stand in the way of true love," she quipped. "Derek and Emma have been invited to a sleepover on Friday night. Why don't you taking her out then? With the kids gone, I wouldn't slap a curfew on you."

He laughed. "Good idea. I could arrange a date." He paused. "What will you do?"

She didn't want to think about the long hours she'd face in her apartment, but whether he brought his date here or to his own house, she definitely wouldn't stick around to meet her.

"Girl things," she answered promptly, thinking she was overdue for a facial and a long bubble bath complete with candles, soft music, and a romance novel.

"I see. Then I'll plan my evening."

"Yes, do." She pasted a smile on her face, painfully aware of unreasonable jealousy gripping her soul.

Christy touched the homemade beer-and-cucumber mask she'd applied to her face and decided it was time to wash off the residue. As Friday night activities went, indulging in a facial wasn't high on the excitement meter, but her pores said it was long overdue. Although her great-grandmother's recipe probably didn't have any real scientific basis for giving a peaches-and-cream complexion, knowing she was one of a long line of women in her family to engage in the ritual was comforting.

Tonight, more than ever, she needed to feel as if she weren't alone.

Puréeing the cucumbers and blending in the other ingredients had also given her something to concentrate on other than Linc's date.

Ever since she'd dropped off the children at their friends' house—fortunately Derek and Emma's buddies were a brother and sister—her thoughts had drifted in a most fruitless direction. It was too easy to create a mental minute-by-minute scenario of Linc's evening.

He *should* spend time with the woman who'd caught his eye, she told herself fiercely. She *should* be happy because he'd finally realized his work was a cold-hearted mistress and was seeking one of flesh and blood. If she'd convinced him to stop postponing his plans for his personal life, then she should pride herself for nudging him along.

Vowing to find a constructive activity, she'd tried to read two different books, but neither held her interest.

She'd lounged on her postage-stamp-sized balcony to enjoy the fall weather and the last few rays of direct sunlight in the quietness, but even nature conspired against her. Birds called to their mates, crickets answered each other's chirps, and the distant sound of children laughing only emphasized her loneliness.

She'd also considered whipping up a batch of cookies, but couldn't because her cupboards were literally bare. Although running into Linc and his date at the grocery store was highly unlikely, she didn't want to risk it.

For a woman who didn't want romance, who was positive she hadn't found a man strong enough to cope with her uncertain future, she was acting completely ridiculously.

She shook off her gloom with great force of will and planned the rest of the evening. As soon as she finished her beauty treatment and slipped on her running shoes, she would take Ria for a romp around the park. By the time they came home, she'd be too tired to imagine what Linc might or might not be doing.

Not knowing was part of her problem, she decided with some irritation. She'd pressed him for details about his prospective girlfriend and his itinerary, aware that asking was similar to probing a sore tooth, but he'd been remarkably uncommunicative.

"I'll leave it up to her," had been his reply, so she'd finally held her questions. Yet she hadn't stopped wondering...

She hoped his mystery woman deserved him.

The doorbell—and Ria's answering barks—interrupted her thoughts. She was inclined to ignore her unexpected visitor, but Ria bounded into the bathroom and began barking in her familiar follow-me style.

"Okay, okay," she grumbled as she patted her face dry, hoping she'd removed all traces of crustiness and didn't smell as if she'd fallen into a distillery vat.

Ria nudged her toward the stairs and stood beside Christy as she unlocked the door.

The man on the stoop caught her by surprise. "Linc!" she exclaimed. "What are you doing here?"

"May I come in?"

"Certainly." She stepped aside, both happy and puzzled that he'd dropped by. "Where's your date? Or should I ask *when* is your date?"

His grin was broad as his gaze traveled down her entire body. A second later, he flicked at a dried flake on her T-shirt. "I came to pick her up, but I'd say she isn't ready."

Her heart pounded and she couldn't breathe. "You came for *me*? But…"

"You're my date." His mouth curled with amusement. "Now, run along and get dressed. I'll occupy Ria's attention so she won't hide your shoes."

Shock, as well as suspicion that she'd somehow misunderstood, had rooted her feet to the floor. "You mean…*I'm* your mystery woman?"

He nodded.

"*I'm* the woman you want to get to know?"

"Yes."

Although her spirits wanted to soar into the stratosphere, she held a tight rein on them. "I don't understand. I thought you cared about…"

"Someone else?" he supplied helpfully.

She hesitated. "Well, yes."

"You were wrong. There isn't anyone else. *You're* the one I care about—the one I want to spend my evening with."

She wanted to cry tears of joy as well as frustration. "You shouldn't want that—"

"Of course I should," he interrupted. "You're a kind, generous, thoughtful woman and every bachelor I know would trade places with me in an instant."

"It's a nice thought, but—"

"Whatever has happened in the past or will happen in the future doesn't matter. The current moment is what we have, so we're going to focus on it. The real question is, have you eaten yet or…" he leaned closer to sniff "…have you been drinking your dinner?"

Her face warmed. "I suspect the ingredients in my great-grandmother's facial recipe were chosen for their, shall we say, *medicinal* qualities." She grinned. "According to Grandma Nell, her mother faithfully applied her facial every Saturday night. Her private time probably included sampling the ingredients while she pampered her skin."

He chuckled. "I don't blame her. Life was hard a hundred years ago and she probably deserved a beer or two at the end of her week."

She smiled. "It makes for an interesting story, doesn't it?" Then, because she didn't want to think about not having descendants who could pass on the tale, she changed the subject. "As for dinner, I haven't eaten."

"Good, because I'm starved. Now, put on your glad rags and let's go."

She should protest, and she was inclined to do so, but she didn't. Perhaps she held back because he acted more like a friend than a guy who was seriously intent on a commitment. Maybe it was only because she was relieved she didn't have to share him with anyone else. She was certainly flattered he'd asked *her* when he could have chosen from a host of eligible women.

It was also far too easy to remind herself she was mere weeks away from her five-year check-up and the end of her self-imposed moratorium on romantic relationships. She could go out, keep the mood light, and just enjoy being in the company of a handsome fellow.

The more she considered, the more enticing an evening of Linc's undivided attention sounded.

"Casual, I assume?" she asked, eyeing his jeans and noticing how fantastic he looked in denim and a cotton shirt.

"Whatever's comfortable," he agreed. "Keep in mind it'll be cool after dark."

She changed in record speed, although she was so excited it took her three tries to successfully brush on her mascara and apply lip gloss.

"I'm ready," she said breathlessly when she emerged fifteen minutes later, wearing her favorite low-cut jeans, a sleeveless white cotton shell and her favorite pearl earrings.

He held out his arm. "Then shall we?"

Before she could pat Ria one final time, he snapped his fingers. "Let's go, Ria."

The dog raced to the door while Christy stared at him. "We're taking her with us?"

"Not to dinner. We'll drop her off at my place on the way. She can chase rabbits and hunt squirrels while we're gone."

"She could stay here. She's used to being alone."

"She could," he agreed, "but wouldn't you rather let her run in a huge yard instead of relegating her to a tiny apartment? Do you really want to deprive her of one of our rare days of nice weather?"

She couldn't refute his argument, although he obviously intended to end up at his place at some point. Was he giving her the opportunity to spend the night by ensuring she couldn't use Ria as an excuse to refuse?

He must have read her mind because he pulled her close. "Before you get all righteous and accuse me of having an ulterior motive, I want you to remember this. However long our night lasts, whether it ends at ten o'clock or in the wee hours, nothing will happen that both of us aren't ready for."

She knew he wouldn't push her beyond her comfort zone—he wasn't the sort who notched his bedposts—but nevertheless she had to ask. "You won't be disappointed if we have an early night?"

His smile was tender as he cupped her face. "I'm a guy. Of course I'd be disappointed, but tonight isn't about me. Tonight is for you."

He was being so sweet, she wanted to cry. More than that, though, she wanted him to kiss her. He obviously wanted it too because he bent his head and she felt his breath brush against the bridge of her nose. Unfortunately, in that split second before his lips met hers, Ria barked impatiently.

He grinned and instead of the lingering kiss he'd been so obviously prepared to give, he delivered a swift peck on her cheek. "We're being paged, so hold that thought."

She did.

CHAPTER EIGHT

"THANKS for letting me share your dinner," Christy said as ninety minutes later they left Rosa's Italian Eatery, the mom-and-pop restaurant he favored for its authentic cuisine and intimate dining atmosphere.

"You're welcome." He'd never divided his dinner with a date before, but Christy had eyed his chicken and eggplant parmesan with such curiosity that he'd given her a sample. In the interest of fairness, she'd shared a taste of her vegetable lasagna and before he knew it, they'd split both meals between them.

"How long have you known Rosa and her husband?" she asked.

He thought for a minute. "Several years. I first met them when their sixteen-year-old son, Frank Junior, had been in a car accident. After I put him back together, Rosa insisted on showing her gratitude by catering a meal for my office staff.

The food was fabulous and now, if I want Italian food, her place is at the top of my list."

She stopped in her tracks and he felt her gaze. "You really amaze me," she said.

He grinned, pleased she was seeing him as a good guy and not of the same ilk as the infamous Jon. "Why? Because I prefer eating at great places?"

"No, because your patients aren't just patients. The ones I've met have always spoken highly of you, and I'd assumed it was because of your surgical skills and the stories of how, no matter how busy you are, you find time to see someone who needs you."

"I try," he admitted, "but I have a few favorites, as I'm sure you do, too."

"Yes, but, unlike you, I don't usually see them again."

They'd reached the car and because Linc had been keeping tabs on the weather, he noticed a bank of clouds building in the west.

"Looks like the weatherman might be right about the rain," she commented.

"That's what I was afraid of."

"Oh? You don't want the moisture? For shame,

Dr Maguire. Don't let the farmers hear you utter such blasphemy," she teased.

"I don't want it *tonight*," he corrected. "I need nice weather for what I had planned."

"Then you *did* organize your evening," she accused good-naturedly. "You told me you were allowing your date to plan your activities."

He grinned. "I did, more or less. She told me what she'd like to do and I took her suggestions to heart."

"I didn't give you any suggestions."

"If I recall, you mentioned Grant's Point."

Her face lit up like the mall's Christmas tree. "Is that where we're going? I can't believe you remembered."

"You'd be amazed at what I remember," he said lightly. In fact, he remembered a lot more than she thought he did. "The only problem is…" he pointed to the sky "…we won't have much time out there before we get wet."

"Bummer."

"Yeah, but if you're okay with waiting, we'll save that excursion for next time." It was a subtle mention of his intention to take her out again, and he waited for her reply.

"I'd like that."

Hiding his satisfaction over her response, he helped her into the car, then walked around to the driver's side.

So far, everything was turning out better than he'd hoped. He'd worried how Christy would react when he arrived on her doorstep unannounced and had half expected her to refuse to go at all. She'd seemed determined to shun a personal relationship until she'd reached the magical date she'd set, which was why he'd used the just-friends approach.

However, his ultimate goal was to show her that friendship would never be enough. For himself, he already wanted more because he didn't want to return to his previous life when everything he did revolved around his work. He wanted his days—his future—revolving around her because he couldn't imagine facing a day without her.

A short time later, Linc escorted Christy into his house and once again she was filled with a sense of belonging, as if she "fit" in this house. If she'd had the finances, not to mention the time and strength, to maintain a place like his, she'd buy it. Her feelings had nothing to do with the owner.

Oh, who was she kidding? She enjoyed being

around Linc whether they were at the hospital, Gail and Ty's house, or his place. If the truth were told, she enjoyed being with him far more than she should at this point in her life.

She paused in front of the patio door. "I'll get Ria so we can go."

"How about a glass of wine first?"

She hesitated. Returning to her empty house wasn't nearly as attractive as staying here with Linc, but, given how easily she was falling for him, it wasn't wise to stay.

"I bought this bottle specifically for our star-gazing," he coaxed. "We may not be able to see too many stars from my patio, but we can't let it go to waste."

Rather than argue that a sealed bottle of wine would keep indefinitely, she gave in because deep down she wanted to stay and pretend she possessed a future as secure as any other twenty-eight-year-old woman's. "One glass, on the patio, please."

If she'd refused, she was certain he would have been chivalrous and obliged, but his broad smile suggested her answer had pleased him. He grabbed two wine glasses and the bottle he'd brought in from the car then accompanied her outdoors.

As soon as she stepped outside and called for Ria, the Lab raced toward them, only to stop abruptly in front of Linc and nudge his leg in an apparent attempt to receive his personal attention, too.

He laughed as he tucked the wine bottle under one arm, then obliged. He'd obviously found the right spot because the dog extended her neck as if to encourage him to shower his attention over a much larger area.

"Don't I get a hello?" she asked her pet lightly, disappointed Ria had transferred her allegiance to Linc so quickly.

Ria wagged her tail and continued to lean into Linc's touch.

"Apparently not," he said. "You know I can find the right spots, don't you, girl?"

"Yes, well, you're going to spoil her with those magic fingers of yours." Remembering his touch on several occasions, she wished she was on the receiving end instead of her dog. "Ria," she asked, "are you almost ready to go home?"

A rabbit darted across the yard and slipped through a small opening in the wooden fence.

Ria gave a sharp woof before bounding to the same corner to nose the ground where her prey had escaped.

"I think her answer was 'No'," Linc said as he handed her an empty glass, then popped the cork on the bottle.

"You do realize she'll be willing to spend hours in your yard?"

He grinned. "She's a dog. Of course she will."

"Yes, but we shouldn't wear out our welcome."

"You won't," he assured her. "If the weather hadn't interfered with my original plan, she'd be spending hours doing what she's doing now."

"Yes, but—"

"Do you have something special to do when you get home?"

"No," she said slowly. "But—"

"But nothing," he said as he poured both glasses half-full. "We may have postponed our Grant's Point trip, but the evening is still ours. *And…*" he emphasized the word "…I have a Plan B."

"Which is?" She sipped her wine.

"We haven't practiced our dance steps today," he reminded her.

"No, we haven't, but one day won't matter."

He lifted an eyebrow. "Speak for yourself, my dear."

She smiled at his grumble. "Mario was quite impressed with you at our last lesson."

"And I want him to stay that way. Or are you trying to get me in trouble with the teacher?"

She laughed. "I can't believe you ever got in trouble at school."

"Contrary to what you might think, I had my moments of infamy. Unfortunately, my stories can't leave this property. They would ruin the 'perfect son' standard I projected to Ty and my sister." He grinned.

She laughed. "I promise. What did you do?"

"Nothing malicious. Mostly stuff like hiding red pens on test days, rearranging the books on the teacher's desk, hiding the dry-erase markers in another classroom so she couldn't post assignments on the board."

"Did your ploys work?"

"Once," he admitted, "but my teachers were a wily bunch. They kept extra red pens and markers in their file cabinets. If one disappeared, they simply pulled another one from their stash or borrowed from another instructor." He smiled. "But my tactics gave us a few minutes' reprieve and to an eight-year-old a few minutes' delay was a coup."

"Did you go to school in Levitt Springs?"

He shook his head. "We grew up about three hours from here. Fortunately, my hometown had a college, so I earned my undergrad degree while Ty and my sister finished high school. After that, we went our separate ways. I began med school, Ty and Joanie entered different colleges and Gran had died by then, so splitting up was inevitable. We kept in touch with weekly phone calls, though."

"How did you and Ty both land in Levitt Springs?"

"Ty had gotten a job with an architecture firm here after he finished his education. Eventually, after I'd completed my surgery residency, I looked for a place to go. I'd narrowed my job offers down to two—one in St. Louis and one here."

"And you chose Levitt Springs."

"My niece and nephew swayed my decision," he admitted. "They don't have grandparents, so it seemed important to give them a doting uncle. I would have moved to be near my sister, too, but she's a buyer for a department-store chain and spends most of her life on the road."

"A win-win situation for everyone," she remarked.

"It is," he agreed. "Being surrounded by family after all those years of only getting together for Memorial Day or Christmas is wonderful. Of course, I'm busy enough that I don't see Ty and his kids as often as I'd like, but we manage to get together at least once a week, even if only for an hour or so."

"Family means a great deal to you," she guessed.

"It does. Although I've watched the kids before on weekends, filling in for Ty makes me eager to have a Derek and Emma of my own."

In another lifetime she would have been thrilled to hear him confirm that his philosophy mirrored hers. However, her future was too uncertain to rejoice in those similarities.

She drained her glass because she couldn't think of a suitable reply.

"More wine?" he asked.

"No, thanks. Our steps are difficult enough without having impaired coordination."

He rose to click a button on his iPod player. The music began and he smiled at her. "Shall we start?"

Regardless of what her future held, her heart

skipped with excitement as she set her glass on the end table and walked into his outstretched arms. "Of course."

For the next thirty minutes she turned and twirled, conscious of his strength as he caught her. Occasionally he stepped on her toes or she stepped on his but as time went on, those incidents occurred less and less.

Finally, they'd managed to make it through the first half of their routine without a single misstep.

"Are we getting good or was that a fluke?" she teased him.

"I vote we try once more," he told her.

So he started the music once again.

To Christy's delight, they repeated their steps perfectly, ending with a final spin that required him to catch her.

For a long minute he simply held her against him, making her aware of how his labored breathing matched hers.

The patter-patter of rain on the roof punctuated the silence and the fresh, clean scent it brought mingled with Linc's masculine fragrance. He exuded warmth, and while that was pleasant, as the air suddenly carried a coolness she hadn't noticed before, she was more impressed by his strength and rock-solidness.

In that instant Linc no longer seemed like a friendly dance partner. He was an attractive, virile man in the prime of his life.

She should push herself away, but she couldn't. The intensity in his gaze was too mesmerizing and savoring this moment too important for her to move.

"That was awesome," he murmured.

"Oh, yes." She didn't know if her breathlessness was due to physical exertion or from being in his arms. She was playing with fire, but it had seemed like for ever since she'd felt as carefree and as attractive as she did at this moment.

It was also a bittersweet moment. She hated to be realistic with romance simmering in the air but she had to control her attraction because these feelings could never grow. Not yet, anyway, and, depending on her doctor's findings, maybe never.

"I suppose we should stop practicing while we're ahead," she said lightly. "End the session on a high note, so to speak."

"Probably."

Yet for the next sixty seconds he didn't release her and she didn't push the issue. The moment would end soon enough and she wanted to enjoy it for as long as it lasted.

"It's raining," she commented inanely, wishing she could go back to her carefree youth when the *C* word only applied to other people. "We should call Ria and go inside."

"I'd rather kiss you," he said.

Her gaze landed on his mouth and although her small voice cautioned her about the wisdom of it, she raised her chin to meet his lips in a kiss so fierce her toes curled and her inner core ached.

"We shouldn't do this," she murmured when he gentled his mouth and inched his way to the sensitive area behind her ear.

"Of course we should."

Her mind barely registered his words, she was too consumed with the sensation of being pressed against his entire length to make sense of them.

Suddenly he pulled away just enough to meet her gaze. The hunger in his expression warmed her down her to her toes. "Have you thought about what we'll do after Gail and Ty return?"

"The Fall Festival is the same day," she pointed out. "The next afternoon I leave for Seattle so I can be bright-eyed and bushy-tailed for my doctor's appointment on that Monday. With a hectic schedule like that, I haven't thought past that weekend."

"We should," he said.

Instinctively, she sensed he was referring to a topic she'd been purposely avoiding. "I imagine we'll go back to the way things were before," she said lightly. "We'll see each other a few times a week at the hospital."

"I don't think so. Too much has changed."

He had a point. Between their shared parenting responsibilities and the dance competition, whenever she saw him on her unit, she treated him differently. Oh, she still gave him the respect he deserved, but now she joked and teased and asked personal questions that she'd never had the courage to ask before. He'd also loosened up enough to join in staff conversations without prompting. Rose hadn't been the only person who'd noticed the change.

"You're right. Things are different. In fact, *you're* so different that several single women have mentioned they'd love to go out with you. If you like, I can give you their names."

She struggled to make the offer because she felt rather possessive about him, but she had no right to that particular feeling. Yes, she'd dragged him out of his shell and convinced him to stop putting his professional career ahead of his personal life, but those lessons would simply prepare him for the woman of his dreams. When he found her and eventually had his own Derek and Emma, and maybe even a Nick or a Beth, she could take pride in the role she'd played.

"You're pulling my leg, right?"

"Not at all. Theresa in Respiratory Therapy, Monica in the Recovery Room, and—"

His hold around her waist tightened. "Their names don't matter because every one of them will be disappointed. Maybe you didn't hear me when I came by your house. I want to spend my time with you—no one else."

It was a wonderful thought and her heart did a happy dance, but the implications scared her. He was asking too much, too soon. "That's sweet of you to say, but—"

"I know you're worried about your upcoming appointment but, whatever happens, I'm not going anywhere. I'll be with you every step of the way."

Christy stiffened, and Linc sensed her mental withdrawal. Any second she'd bolt, and he imperceptibly tightened his hold. She felt too good right where she was and he wanted to show her both literally and figuratively that he wouldn't let her go without a fight.

There would be no turning back.

He could have said nothing and let the days roll by, but she needed to know that *this* time she wouldn't face her future with only Ria as her companion. His intentions were to prove he had more staying power and more strength of character than the other jerks who had walked into—and out of—her life.

Moisture glistened in her eyes and she blinked rapidly. "I know you mean well, but please don't make any promises."

"I already have."

"I won't hold you to them," she warned.

"Are you giving me an escape clause?"

"Someone has to."

"Do you really think I'm the sort of guy who runs at the first sign of trouble?"

Her shoulders slumped before she shook her head. "No, but it's too risky to say what you might do when or if the situation changes."

He disagreed, but she wouldn't change her opinion in the space of this conversation. "Okay." He spoke evenly. "We'll continue our discussion after your appointment, but I happen to believe we have a future. Don't let fear hold you hostage."

For a long minute she didn't move, until finally she nodded ever so slightly. "I'll try."

Pleased by his small victory, he stepped forward and lightly brushed her cheekbone with his lips. "That's all I ask."

At times over the next three weeks Christy wondered if she'd imagined that particular conversation because Linc never referred to it again. However, every now and then she'd catch him studying her, sometimes with curiosity and sometimes with a speculative gleam, but no matter what she saw in his eyes, he always smiled his lazy grin that turned her insides to mush. She tried to do as he'd asked—to think about a life after she received her five-year medical report—and it was easy when he was nearby. In the wee hours of the night, however, when darkness had closed in and she had only Ria to hold her fears at bay, it wasn't. Fortunately, those instances didn't happen often. She was simply too busy trying to stay on top of their schedule and keep the household running smoothly to reflect past the upcoming weeks.

Time, however, was marching on and the kitchen calendar reflected it. Emma had circled the date of her parents' return with a red magic marker and, thanks to the huge black Xs she marked in the squares at the end of each day, Christy could count the remaining white spaces at a glance.

There were fourteen of them.

Her time of sharing the house with Linc and playing a mother's role was drawing to a close, so she savored every moment, including those less than idyllic times…

"Christy." Derek raced into the kitchen while she was finishing the dinner dishes. "Emma keeps bugging me. She won't stay out of my room."

"He took my doll's car," Emma wailed, "and I know he's hiding it under his bed. I want it back."

"I didn't take it. It's probably buried under all your doll junk." His disgust was obvious.

"My stuff is *not* junk." Emma's lower lip quivered.

"Is, too."

"Is not."

"Guys," Christy warned. "Both of you, calm down."

"He called my stuff *junk*." Emma was clearly affronted. "I don't make fun of his toys." She poked a finger in her brother's chest. "Take that back."

"Will not. And quit touching me."

He shoved his sister and Emma began weeping. "You're being mean. I want my mommy! She'd make you be nice to me!"

Christy abandoned her task to hold the little girl as she sobbed on her shoulder. "Oh, sweetie, your mom will be home in two weeks. That's only fourteen days. Don't forget about tonight being our phone call night. You don't want your mom and dad to see you with red eyes and a runny nose, do you?"

Emma sniffled.

"You're just being a baby," Derek complained in a typical big-brother voice.

"Am not!"

"Stop, you two," Christy scolded. "We'll straighten this out in a few minutes."

Linc had been outside watering the shrubs and walked in as Christy delivered her warning.

"What's going on?" he asked.

Emma pointed a finger at her brother. "He started it."

"Did not."

"Quiet. Both of you," Linc ordered. "Will someone tell me what's going on?"

"Emma can't find her doll's car and she thinks Derek took it," Christy explained.

"I didn't," Derek insisted.

"Did, too!"

Linc held up his hands. "There's only one way to solve this. We'll look for the car right now."

"It's in Derek's room," Emma informed them.

"Is not."

Christy exchanged a glance at Linc over their heads and shrugged. "They've been like this all afternoon."

"Off you go to your rooms," he commanded as he pointed. "I'll be there in a minute."

As each child stormed to their private corners, Linc paused. "All this drama is over a lost car?"

"That convertible is very important to Em," Christy said with a smile. "The main problem is they both miss their parents. She reacts with tears and Derek hides his feelings behind aggression."

"I didn't realize. Everything was going so smoothly I'd hoped we'd passed that stage."

"We did, but two months can seem like for ever to a child. A time out for both is in order, I think."

A distant door slammed and Christy smiled. "Do you want to deal with that or should I?"

"I will," he said.

He returned less than ten minutes later. "The mystery of the missing car is solved."

"Where was it?"

"Under Emma's bed. She'd decided the space was the perfect place for a 'garage' and forgot. She apologized to Derek, so life is good."

"Will you be able to handle them by yourself tomorrow?"

"Considering they'll be in school most of the day, I'd say so," he said wryly, "but I've been thinking. I could go with you."

His offer surprised her because when she'd mentioned her upcoming trip a week ago, he'd simply nodded. "I'm flying to Seattle for the usual battery of tests, not open-heart surgery. Don't you have patients to see?"

"None that couldn't wait until next week," he said. "I've been rearranging my schedule, just in case."

"You have?" She could hardly believe he'd go to the trouble. "Whatever for? You'd go crazy sitting in waiting rooms all day."

He grinned. "Probably, but I'd do it. For moral support."

She wanted to cry at his thoughtfulness. "Thanks, but my mom has planned to spend the day with me. She's used to the routine."

"Good, because I don't want you to be alone," he stated firmly.

It seemed strange to have someone other than her own family fuss over her. His concern gave her a warm, fuzzy feeling that was far better than hot cocoa and a warm blanket on a cold winter night.

"I won't be," she assured him. "This way is best for the kids, too. After tonight's outburst, they need you, not a sitter."

"Maybe, but I still don't understand why you want to travel so far for your tests, only to turn around in another two weeks to visit your doctor. We run the same procedures here, you know."

His voice and expression revealed his frustration quite clearly and she tried to explain her reasons. "This seems silly, but all my records are there and I'd like to have the same people looking at my scans. As crazy as it sounds, they've given me good reports and I don't want to jinx myself."

He fell silent for a few seconds before he finally nodded. "If that's what you need for peace of mind, then that's what you should do."

She was half-surprised he didn't try to convince her otherwise. "You aren't going to tell me I'm being illogical and superstitious?"

"I could," he admitted, "but having faith in one's medical team is crucial to a patient's recovery. If you aren't ready for someone else to run your tests, you shouldn't. Otherwise, whatever the outcome, you'll always question the results."

"Thanks for understanding."

"What I don't like is how you're going to be exhausted when you return."

"It's sweet of you to worry, but I'll be fine."

He frowned. "I don't see how you will be. You're taking the red-eye flight in the morning, spending the entire day being poked, prodded and scanned, then jetting back late at night. At least stay a little longer and fly home Saturday."

"I scheduled my flights months ago. I can't change them now without huge penalties."

"Screw the penalties. I'll pay the difference."

"I can't have you do that. Honestly, I'll be fine." She grinned. "Keep the light on for me, okay?"

"I'll do better than that. I'll be waiting up."

CHAPTER NINE

CHRISTY kissed her mother on the cheek as soon as she met her at the baggage claim the next morning. "Hi, Mom. It's great to see you."

"You, too, hon," her mother said. At a very young-looking fifty-four, Serena Michaels was dressed fashionably smart in spite of the early hour and their final destination. Although Christy had told her repeatedly that no one expected her to look as if she was heading for a photo shoot instead of a day at the hospital, her mother had disagreed.

"If you look great, you'll feel great, too," had been her mantra, so Christy had taken a few special pains herself. Instead of wearing blue jeans and a T-shirt, she'd worn a comfortable pair of dress slacks, one of her favorite designer shirts, and a matching sweater.

"Did you have a good flight?"

"No problems," she answered cheerfully, preparing for the inevitable question that would come next.

"How are you feeling?"

She'd trained herself over the years to not worry about cancer invading again if she didn't feel well, but her mother hadn't learned the same lesson. She still needed the reassurance that as long as her daughter felt healthy, then it must be so.

"Never better," Christy answered. "I really appreciate you taking the time away from the restaurant today."

"Of course I'd take the day off," Serena assured her as she ushered her to the parking garage. "We may as well use the time in between your tests to catch up. I want to hear all about your side job as a live-in nanny and this dance competition you've told me about."

While Christy filled in the details, she soaked up the ambience of the city. She'd grown up here, and while it was home, it also wasn't. Oddly enough, she felt more rooted in Levitt Springs and she wondered if Linc had made the difference.

Throughout the day Christy shared story after story between her sessions of blood draws, PET and bone-density scans, and every other test her physician had ordered. She didn't realize Linc had figured prominently in every tale until her mother commented.

"You've talked about this Linc a lot lately. Is he someone new?"

"I've been acquainted with him since I moved to town, but I didn't really *know* him until we began taking care of his brother's children."

"He sounds like a special fellow," Serena remarked.

"He is. He even offered to rearrange his patient schedule to come with me today."

A knowing smile appeared on her mother's face. "He's that taken with you, is he?"

"He seems to be, but..." she hesitated "...I'm not sure it's wise."

"Why not? You're healthy, attractive, and—" Serena stopped short. "You've told him about your history, haven't you?"

"Yes, Mother."

"The news didn't scare him away?"

"It should have," she said honestly, still amazed by his tenacity, "but it hasn't so far."

Serena's eyes glowed with happiness and she leaned over to hug her. "You're going to keep him, aren't you?"

"A relationship isn't that simple for me, Mom. There are long-term consequences to consider."

"He's a physician, Christy. Of course he knows the consequences."

"I'm just trying to protect him from making a mistake he'll regret, especially if my ovaries never wake up and he can't have the son or daughter he wants."

"I may not be in the medical profession, but even I know there are plenty of ways around that particular problem. Do you love him?"

Christy pondered for a moment. Her feelings for Linc were much stronger and deeper than those she'd felt toward Jon, but she wasn't ready to admit she was in love.

"I care about him," she said simply. "More than I'd expected I would. Probably even more than I should, which is why I can't be certain he really knows what he's getting into. Yes, he has all the medical knowledge, but I'm not sure his heart knows what he's getting into."

"You want to protect him."

Linc had called her tactic "giving him an escape clause". However anyone described it, her mother had pegged her correctly.

"Yes."

"You can be right about so many things, but in this you're wrong. Call your excuse for what it is, daughter. You're not trying to protect him as much as you're trying to protect yourself."

Christy mentally argued against that notion throughout the day, but by the time she was back on the plane and flying home, she finally conceded her mother's assessment might have merit.

She'd always thought she was being altruistic by spelling everything out early in her relationships. Full disclosure early on was in everyone's best interests because if a fellow couldn't deal with her situation, she'd rather learn it early in a relationship. Maybe she *was* only protecting herself, but her method worked.

With Linc, however, it hadn't. He wasn't reacting true to form.

I'll be with you every step of the way, he'd told her. She wanted to believe him, but she couldn't take that leap of faith. He was the one man who, if he ever changed his mind and walked away, would devastate her to the point where she'd never recover.

As the evening dragged on and bad weather

delayed her flight, one thought kept her going—
she was heading home.

As the hours ticked by, Linc found it more and
more difficult to wait patiently for Christy's return. Every light in the main part of the house
blazed because he wanted her to see the beacon
as soon as she turned onto their street.

He'd expected her at nine and wished he could
have met her at the airport, but he couldn't leave
Derek and Emma unattended. He'd tried phon-
ing her, but his call had gone straight to her voice
mail. A check on her flight status via the internet
told him she'd been delayed due to bad weather.
He might have wished the airline had cancelled
the flight so she wouldn't endure such a long
travel day, but he wanted her safe at home and
he wouldn't rest until she was.

Finally, he heard the distinctive sound of the garage door mechanism and his shoulders slumped
with relief.

"You made it," he said inanely as he greeted her
with a heartfelt hug and a brief kiss.

"Finally," she muttered. Her body drooped with
apparent exhaustion, her smile seemed forced,
and she leaned on him as if the sheer act of stand-

ing required more energy than she could summon. She made no effort to leave his embrace, which suited him just fine.

"It's past midnight. I can't believe you waited up for me. You didn't have to, but I'm glad you did."

He grinned. Those few words made the hours of impatience worth it. "I said I would. I couldn't go back on my word, could I?" he said lightly, hoping she'd see this incident as another example of his trustworthiness. "I couldn't sleep anyway until you got home."

She chuckled. "I'll bet you stayed awake when Ty or your sister went out, too."

"Sometimes," he admitted, although waiting for his siblings didn't compare to waiting for Christy. Not knowing where she was or what might be happening had made it impossible to close his eyes. The saying "Ignorance is bliss" didn't apply where Christy was concerned.

He changed the subject. "How did your tests go?"

"Like they usually do. I didn't do a thing except lie on the X-ray tables or sit in chairs. Machines and the staff did all the work."

"Are you tired?" he asked, already knowing the answer.

"Very. You'd think, though, after sitting or lying down all day, I wouldn't be."

"It's a good thing tomorrow is Saturday," he told her. "The kids and I will watch cartoons so you can sleep late."

"That isn't necessary," she began.

"Yes, it is," he insisted. "I'm repaying the favor."

As a sign of her exhaustion, she capitulated. "Okay, but no later than nine," she warned. "Derek has a soccer game at eleven and I have a few things to do before then."

"Nine a.m.," he repeated. "Can I get you anything now? A cup of herbal tea? A glass of water?"

"No, thanks."

"Okay, then. Pleasant dreams."

"You, too," she murmured, before disappearing into her room.

As he performed his final walk-through of the house for the night, his own exhaustion tugged at him and he realized he was ready for the day to end. Now, though, it could, because Christy had come home.

Christy didn't report to work until Tuesday, but the thought of what Linc and the children had done for her this past weekend still brought a smile to her face. Promptly at nine a.m. on Saturday, Emma had knocked on her door and Linc had barged in, carrying a breakfast tray. The plate had contained several misshapen pancakes, a small bowl of fresh strawberries and blueberries, and a cup of her favorite herbal tea prepared specially for her by Emma.

The day had been declared a "Coddle Christy" day and the trio had done so with great enthusiasm. She'd been encouraged to do nothing but eat and sleep and although she'd been certain she didn't need a nap, she'd found herself snoozing in Linc's lounge chair when they'd gone to his house to water his flowers.

His thoughtfulness had given her a few bittersweet moments because their time of sharing a house would be ending soon. While it wouldn't be long before she'd only have her memories to sustain her, what fun it was to create them.

Her good mood faded, however, as Linc pulled her and her supervisor, Denise, into a treatment room during his morning rounds and closed the door.

"I want Christy to look after Mrs Connally this week," he informed Denise in his typical, authoritative physician's voice.

Shocked by his request, Christy listened with a combination of horrified surprise, embarrassment, and anger at his high-handedness. "I appreciate your request, Doctor," the charge nurse said diplomatically, "but I can't honor it. If I allowed the doctors to pick and choose which nurses would look after their patients, I'd have a staffing nightmare."

"It's in Mrs Connally's best interests for Christy to be her nurse," he argued. "Have I ever asked for a favor before?"

"Well, no, but I can't establish a precedent. If the other doctors—or the nurses—learned I gave you a special favor, I've have a mutiny on my hands."

"Who has to know?" he said. "This is strictly between the three of us."

"I realize the medical staff each has his or her favorite nurses, but I work hard to spread the difficult cases around. Christy already has several. I can't load her with one more."

"Then pass one of hers to someone else."

"I could, but why do you want her for this particular case?" Denise asked, ever blunt. "I have more experienced nurses—"

"This woman and her family need Christy right now."

"I don't understand."

"You don't have to. However, I know what I'm talking about."

Denise frowned. "I'm sorry, but if you want me to bend the rules, I need a good reason to do so. Why is Christy the only nurse who can take care of your post-mastectomy patient?"

Christy's anger and embarrassment faded as the reasons were painfully obvious. To Linc's credit, he didn't divulge her story but simply reiterated his stance.

"Because I believe she is," he said. "Let's leave it at that, shall we?"

Seeing Denise's mulish expression, Christy knew her supervisor wouldn't give in. Linc wasn't trying to draw attention to her but he must be concerned about his patient to ask for such an unusual favor.

"I can explain," she addressed her supervisor quietly. "I had a double mastectomy myself."

Denise's argumentative expression vanished and she looked as shocked as if the floor had disappeared underneath her feet. "You?"

"Yeah. About five years ago."

"My patient needs to see she can still have a full and happy life," Linc added. "Because of her personal experience, Christy can show her that in a way few others can."

Denise let out a deep breath. "Okay. You've been reassigned. Tanya can take Mr Wiseman." She paused, peering over her reading glasses. "You should have told me about this before now."

She shrugged. "I've told a few of my patients if they've had similar surgeries, but I didn't necessarily want it to be common knowledge."

"You do realize I'll take advantage of your experience in the future, don't you?"

Christy nodded. "Yes, ma'am."

"Then it's settled." Denise addressed Linc. "Are you satisfied, Doctor?"

He worked his mouth in an obvious attempt to hide a grin. "Absolutely."

"Good." Denise strode from the room, leaving Christy alone with Linc.

"I'm sorry for putting you on the spot," he began, "but Renee Connally is having a difficult time coping with her diagnosis. She's forty years old, has three children, and is convinced her life is over."

"Is it?" she asked.

"The cancer is invasive, but we caught it early and her sentinel lymph nodes are clear. You were the first person I thought of who might convince her that she can get past this. I'm sorry I outed you."

"The news was bound to break sooner or later," she said, "but don't worry about it. Meanwhile, I'll talk to her."

"Thanks," he said. "The sooner you get her to look positively at her future, the better."

Christy found Renee dozing, her husband in the chair beside her bed. As soon as she walked in, the woman opened her eyes.

"I'm Christy and I'll be taking care of you," she said calmly. "Are you staying ahead of your pain?"

"For the most part."

Christy chatted about non-consequential topics while she checked Renee's drain and offered to teach her how to maintain it as soon as Renee was able. After discussing a few other physical issues with her, Christy said cheerfully, "Doctor says we have to get you moving, so I'm going to bump your hubby from his chair. You can sit there for a while."

As her husband jumped up, Renee shook her head. "I'd rather not. There isn't any point, is there?"

"Of course there is. Lying in bed won't help you return to your normal life."

"That's the point. My life isn't normal any more, is it?"

"Not by your old standards, but whatever treatment you face won't last for ever. You're facing a tough period, to be sure, but you can get past this. You have to, for your children's sakes."

"I know you mean well, but save your Pollyanna attitude for someone else. You have no idea what I'm going through."

"Actually, I do," she said bluntly. "I had a double mastectomy five years ago and I'm proof that life goes on." She pulled up a nearby folding chair and began to tell her story.

By the end of the week, Christy was pleased with Renee Connally's progress. She had begun to take an active interest in her own nursing care and her entire outlook seemed much improved.

She'd also learned something from Renee and her husband as well. As she watched her walk the hallway with his help and sometimes caught the two of them in the room with their heads together, she came to a startling conclusion.

Jon hadn't loved her.

Oh, he'd been good company and they'd got along well, but true love had staying power. When the going got tough, love allowed two people to endure. It didn't encourage one person to abandon the other.

I'm not going anywhere.

Linc's words resurfaced in her memory. For the first time she began to believe it was possible—that there *were* men who stood by their wives and girlfriends during difficult times. That fellows like Jon were the exception, not the rule.

Unfortunately, her revelation came at a time when she had to shelve her personal concerns and focus on the job at hand. Gail and Ty were due home on Saturday and Christy had a million things to do before they arrived. Not only was the dance competition on her mind but she wanted everything in the house to be in perfect order, from the housework to the laundry. To that end, she created lists of chores for everyone until Linc complained as loudly as the children.

Naturally, Derek and Emma were wild with anticipation.

"We should visit the park so Ria can run off their energy, shouldn't we?" Linc said on Wednesday evening.

"I think so," she said ruefully. "The sad thing is, they're like Energizer Bunnies. Poor Ria is so tired her tail drags most of the time."

"After Saturday, Ria can resume her quiet life." He paused. "If their flight is delayed again for any reason, we'll cut it close to get to our event on time."

"We'll manage. If nothing else, we'll leave their car and they can drive themselves home."

"Let's hope we don't have to. Derek and Emma would be crushed if they weren't able to greet their parents as soon as they land."

Christy didn't understand what had caused the airline to bump Gail and Ty to a later flight, but she was relieved to have the extra hours' reprieve. Truth was, she wasn't looking forward to returning to her quiet little apartment after being a part of a boisterous family atmosphere.

"I've been spoiled the past two months," Linc commented.

"Spoiled? How?"

"As crazy as it sounds, I liked having all the

commotion when I came home at night. It'll take time to get used to peace and quiet again."

"I agree." She grinned. "Maybe we can borrow Derek and Emma for the occasional weekend."

"It's a deal," he said.

Suddenly both children raced through the house, doors slamming, with Ria barking at their heels as they rushed into the back yard.

Linc visibly winced. "I was going to ask if you wanted to run through our dance routine again, but we'd better save that for later. Unless you think we don't need the practice."

She hated the idea of never dancing with him again, so she intended to make the most of her opportunities.

"'Practice makes perfect,'" she quoted. "I'll pencil you into my schedule after the kids are in bed for the night."

"I can't wait."

Neither, it seemed, could she.

On Saturday at two, Linc herded his group through the airport to the baggage claim where they waited for Gail and Ty to arrive. According to the monitors, their flight would land in a few minutes, so they still had plenty of time to wait.

Linc would have preferred spending the extra hour at the house, but every five minutes Derek or Emma had asked, "Can we leave yet?"

Although he'd miss the time with the children, Linc was glad his brother would be home again. He looked forward to giving Christy his full attention.

"Are you okay?" he asked her as they milled around the open area along with others who were also waiting for their friends and family to appear.

"Sure. Why wouldn't I be?"

He suspected the reason went far beyond her desire to create a perfect homecoming. She'd been in her element taking care of Derek and Emma and she was probably sad because her opportunity would end within the next few minutes. Little did she know, though, that he intended to keep her busier than ever.

"You look a little stressed," he hedged.

"Too much on my mind, I guess. Oh, look." She pointed to the group of passengers descending on them. "They're here."

As both children broke away to run toward their parents, Linc remained at Christy's side, his arm slung around her waist. From the way she swiped at the corner of her eyes, he knew his brother's family reunion bothered her more than she let on.

He remained rooted to the spot, determined to show her that no matter the situation, she could lean on him.

"My word, Christy!" Gail exclaimed as she walked into her house a short time later. "This place looks better than when I left."

Christy laughed at her friend's awe. "I wouldn't go that far, but everyone worked hard to get ready for you. We also went grocery shopping and stocked the refrigerator so you won't have to fight the stores for a few days until you recover from jet lag."

"You've thought of everything," Gail marveled. "So tell me quick while the men are unloading the suitcases—how did things go with you and Linc?"

"Great."

Her gaze narrowed. "You're not just saying that, are you?"

"No, I'm not. In fact, things went much better than I'd ever dreamed they would. You were right. He really is a great guy. In fact, I'll probably miss having him around on a daily basis, dirty socks and all," she finished lightly.

Gail eyed her carefully. "Oh, my gosh. You've fallen in love with him, haven't you?"

Christy wanted to deny it, but she couldn't— not to her dearest friend. She didn't know when it had happened, but it had. "I think so," she said.

"How does he feel?"

She smiled. "He says he isn't going anywhere."

Gail clapped her hands and crowed. "I *knew* you two were meant for each other. This is absolutely *wonderful*."

"No, it isn't," she said flatly. "We have so many potential problems ahead of us. It wouldn't be fair to ask him to face those when he doesn't have to."

"Don't you think he's already weighed the pros and cons? He's an adult and can make his own decisions," Gail informed her. "He doesn't need you to think for him."

"I know, but how can I be sure he won't change his mind when the going gets rough?"

"Some things you have to take on faith."

Unfortunately, when it came to something this important, her faith was practically non-existent.

"Are you worried about your doctor's appointment? Is that why you can't think reasonably?"

"I'm concerned, not worried, and I *am* thinking reasonably."

The sympathy in Gail's eyes suggested that she didn't agree. "You've been feeling okay, haven't you? You don't have any symptoms that you're not telling me about?"

"No symptoms and, yes, Mother, I've been feeling fine. Thanks for asking."

"I'm sounding mother-hen-ish, aren't I?"

"A little, but I know you mean well." She hugged her friend. "I'm glad you're back," she said sincerely, because she *had* missed her. "Thanks again for the opportunity to look after your kids. We had a wonderful time and I'll never forget it."

"I'm glad. We couldn't have enjoyed ourselves as much as we did if we weren't confident Derek and Emma were taken care of."

Linc walked in with a suitcase in each hand, his brother behind him equally laden. "I hate to rush away without hearing about your time in France, but Christy and I have a fall festival to attend."

Gail snapped her fingers. "That's right. The dance competition is tonight. I'd forgotten."

"We haven't, because, oh, by the way, we're going to win." Linc grinned.

Christy laughed. "Spoken like an overconfident surgeon. Seriously, though, we're quite good."

"I left four tickets on the counter if you decide

you'd like to watch our performance," Linc informed his brother and sister-in-law. "We're the very last couple on the schedule, so it'll be close to nine o'clock. After that, the disc jockey will provide music and open the dance floor to everyone."

After a quick round of goodbyes, Christy allowed Linc to escort her and Ria to her car. Her suitcases were already in the trunk and as soon as he opened the passenger door, Ria bounded inside.

"I guess this is it," she said.

"Only for now," he said firmly. "I'll pick you up at your house in two hours. That will give you time to rest before our big evening."

"You mean time to get nervous?"

"You aren't nervous, are you? This can't be coming from the woman who assured me this fundraiser was all in the spirit of fun."

"I lied," she said promptly.

"Surely my fearless partner—the same lady who jumps out of airplanes and rides the rapids—isn't suffering from cold feet, is she?"

"As crazy as it sounds, yes."

"Silly woman," he said with obvious affection. "Win or lose, we're going to be great."

She eyed him carefully. "Somehow I'd always imagined that I'd give *you* the pep talk tonight. Are you the same Lincoln Maguire who had to be coerced into participating?"

"One and the same, but we've practiced until we could both dance our steps in our sleep and sometimes I have. If we trip or miss a step, we've already practiced that, too." He grinned. "We'll recover."

His humor was infectious. "We will, but why don't I save time and meet you at the convention center?"

"I seem to remember having this same discussion once before," he said sternly, although the twinkle in his eye minimized the sting, "but now, like then, my answer is no. We're partners. We'll arrive and leave together."

His description made her realize how badly she needed him to understand what a partnership with her would mean. Somehow she had to make certain he looked at a future through regular lenses and not rose-colored glasses. However, she'd save that discussion for later.

She gave in. "If that's what you want to do."

"It is. Now, drive home safely, and I'll see you soon."

She couldn't stop her pulse from leaping with anticipation, although she knew tonight's dance competition might only be the beginning of the end.

CHAPTER TEN

LINC strode into his house and hardly noticed the quiet. He was too busy replaying the last few hours they'd spent together. From the moment they'd got into the car and headed to the airport, he'd sensed Christy's mental withdrawal. At first, he'd thought it was because she simply didn't want to say goodbye to the kids, but his gut warned that it went much deeper. She intended to distance herself from *him*, probably out of an altruistic notion that she would save him from himself.

He wasn't going to let her because he intended to stick to her like glue. The only way she'd get away from him would be if she moved to another city, and he wasn't averse to following her. In the space of a few weeks he'd come to the point where he wanted her to be a part of his every day. He didn't want some steady, dependable sort, although Christy was all that and more. He wanted the Christy who fearlessly faced life with joy and grace because…

Because he loved her.

The realization hit him hard, but it was true. He loved her, and he'd do anything within his power for her, just as his father had done for the love of *his* life. As he looked at his childhood with new eyes the weight of his old resentments dropped off. He couldn't let the day end without telling Christy how he felt.

She'd probably tell him he was mistaken or try to convince him of her shortcomings, but she didn't understand the most important thing. He needed her just as she was.

They were by no means late and, in fact, had arrived at the convention hall a little early, but Christy was amazed by the crowd of people who'd already gathered.

"You're at table five, near the front," the woman at the check-in desk informed them. "Enjoy yourselves and good luck with the competition. We have a packed house tonight."

The news didn't come as any surprise. Christy had suspected people would come in droves and it was nice to know she'd been right.

"Let's find our table before we mingle," Linc said in her ear because the noise level already made hearing difficult.

"Good idea," she said, conscious of his hand on the small of her back as they wound their way through the tables and groups of people. The skirt of her red silky dress, purchased specifically for tonight's occasion because it flared and flowed in the right places, swung provocatively over her sashaying hips. The spaghetti-strapped bodice was covered in glittery sequins and would sparkle like diamonds under the spotlight. The garment fit perfectly and although Linc's hand didn't stray from the base of her spine, her skin sizzled under the heat of his fingers.

She'd proved her mother's belief about clothing, she decided. She felt as sensational as the dress, and Linc's admiring gaze when he'd arrived at her house had told her it had been money well spent.

Linc had earned her admiring gaze, too. She'd seen him wearing scrubs, casual work attire as well as workout clothes, but, as wonderfully as he filled out those garments, he was positively awesome in his black tuxedo pants and the long-sleeved dress shirt he wore open at his neck.

Christy meandered past various groups and mingled with others, conscious of Linc remaining at her side. She was surprised he didn't veer off to visit with his own friends and colleagues and leave her to her own devices. Instead, if he wanted to speak to someone, he'd grab her hand and drag her along. If she saw someone and headed toward them, he followed.

The truth was she was thrilled he didn't leave her. At this moment they were a couple. A pair. Partners.

I'm not going anywhere, he'd told her on several occasions, and since then he hadn't. For the first time she began to believe that it might be true—that he wouldn't leave her when or if the going got rough.

By the end of the hour the hall was packed and they took their seats at the same table as several of Linc's partners and their wives.

Janice Martin, a distinguished lady in her mid-sixties, who was seated on Christy's left, leaned close. "I'm pleased you convinced Linc to participate in this event. The man is too young to work twenty-four seven. He needed an interest outside the hospital and I'm delighted you gave him one."

"Thank you, but it was more a case of bullying him into it rather than persuading him to volunteer."

Janice patted her arm. "However you managed this miracle, I'm glad you did. Why, he looks like a new man."

Christy glanced at Linc, who was chatting with Dale Zorn, a cardiologist, on his right. The version of the Lincoln Maguire beside her bore little resemblance to the man she'd known a few weeks ago. That fellow had been tense, extremely focused, and didn't smile. Now his face was animated and his body relaxed, as if he didn't have a care in the world.

"Being a temporary father to his nephew and niece had a lot to do with his transformation," she told Janice.

"Ah, yes. My husband told me you two were looking after his brother's kids. How did you enjoy being parents?"

How could she possibly describe the best experience in recent memory? "I had the time of my life," she said simply.

As soon as she'd voiced those words, she realized how appropriate it had been for Linc to choose that particular song for their dance routine. It was a fitting end to their two months together.

Selfishness suddenly reared its head. Because of all the potential obstacles facing them, ending their relationship might be for the best, but every fiber of her being warned that it would be a mistake—one she would regret for the rest of her days. Truth was, she wanted what the Connallys had—a partnership that saw them through the good times as well as the bad.

Their partnership was more than a simple agreement between two people. Love had knit them together; love had made the difference—the same type of love she felt for Linc.

Then you know what you have to do, her little voice chided her. *Take the risk.*

She wanted to ponder her choices and replay all of her what-if scenarios, but the master-of-ceremonies interrupted her thoughts as he began the event. Linc turned to her. "Nervous?"

"A little. You?"

"Never better."

For the next thirty minutes Christy and the rest of the guests were entertained by the various teams who performed. Some were good, others fair, still others were perfectly awful or downright hilarious, but through it all she was conscious of Linc's arm resting on the back of her chair, his hand curled around her shoulder.

She simply couldn't imagine going back to the way things had been before. In the hours prior to tonight's event, her apartment had seemed so sterile and lifeless and the thought of facing that existence day after day was too horrible to imagine.

She wanted to be with Linc, morning, noon, and night. She wanted him to tease her about how she squeezed her toothpaste, rave over her meals, and pamper Ria as much as she did. She needed him in more ways than she could ever list, and she needed him like she needed air to breathe, because she loved him.

So focused was she on her epiphany, she hardly noticed he'd moved until he whispered into her ear, his breath warm against her neck. "We're next."

She nodded. The butterflies in her stomach suddenly settled as she resolved to express her feelings during their song. She realized how diligently he'd been working to convince her to trust him and now seemed the perfect opportunity to show him what lay in her heart. The words would come later, when they were alone.

The performance ended, although Christy had been so focused on her private thoughts she hadn't paid attention to her competition. After the applause died down, the MC announced their names.

Linc grabbed her hand and led her to the dance floor. Before he left her to stand alone center stage, he squeezed her fingers and winked.

She laughed at his irreverence while he moved to stage right. The crowd fell silent as the familiar melody began.

Christy allowed the music to wash over her, paying careful attention to the lyrics as she poured out the emotions that matched those expressed in the song.

Through the basic grind that brought a few cat-calls, then the flamenco, various dips and spins, the spectators faded into nothingness as she focused on Linc.

He clearly did the same because his gaze had locked on hers. Easily, effortlessly, she glided through the steps. As the music drew to a close, the final spin brought her into Linc's embrace.

Barely conscious of the thundering applause, she only had eyes for Linc. He traced her jaw, then bent his head and kissed her in such a lingering manner that her toes tingled and the crowd went wild.

As the announcer came to the microphone, Linc broke contact and they made their way back to their table. Christy's heart pounded as much from his kiss as from the exertion and she felt so marvelous she was certain her feet didn't touch the floor. People nodded to her as they clapped while others pounded Linc on his back for a job well done.

"Okay, folks. Based on the amount of applause, I think it's easy to tell which team is our winner. Dr Lincoln Maguire and his lovely partner, Christy Michaels!"

The hired DJ began a music set and encouraged everyone to participate. The mood in the building was high and from the numbers of couples who took to the dance floor, they'd been energized by Christy and Linc's performance.

"Do you want to stay?" Linc asked her.

She hesitated, trying to read him and failing. "Would you mind if we didn't?"

His slow grin was the answer she wanted. "Not at all."

Although Linc graciously accepted everyone's congratulations on their way out, he chafed at the delay. He wanted to simply toss Christy over his shoulder and walk through the throng, but he'd already pushed his limits when he'd kissed Christy in front of five hundred spectators. People he knew and those he didn't remarked on his memorable performance, although he didn't know if they'd been impressed by his dancing ability or because he'd kissed his partner with such fervor.

Either way, the first *Dancing with the Docs* event would go down in hospital history.

"Would you like to come inside?" she asked as he pulled into a parking space outside her apartment.

"I'd like that." His gut warned him that something monumental would take place and, if his suspicions were correct, it wouldn't be good.

"My selection is limited tonight," she said as she headed for her kitchen. "Would you like water or wine?"

The wine could wait until they had something to celebrate. "Water, please." As she handed him a glass and they headed into the living room, he asked, "What's on your mind? And don't say 'Nothing' because I can read you too well."

"Okay." She placed her glass on the coffee table before she sank onto her sofa. "Here's the deal.

"This afternoon, I'd contemplated how we should go our separate ways."

He nodded. "I suspected as much."

"It seemed the right thing to do. You want things out of life that I might not be able to give you—two point five kids, a minivan, becoming soccer parents, and the potential to celebrate a fiftieth anniversary, to name a few.

"My mother told me I was trying to protect myself from being hurt, and deep down I was. I'd done a good job, too, until you came along," she said wryly, "but you wiggled through my defenses and I did the unthinkable. I fell in love with you."

After bracing himself for the worst, relief swept through him to the point he couldn't speak.

Her mouth trembled as she met his gaze. "Whatever happens next is up to you."

Rather than act on her cue to leave if he so desired, he drew her against him. "I'm not going anywhere."

"You're sure? Think long and hard about your decision," she warned.

"I already have. I love you too much to be intimidated by the obstacles we might face."

Tears glistened in her eyes. "Oh, Linc."

"You should know that I'd anticipated this conversation ever since you left Gail and Ty's. In fact, I'd intended to seduce you if that's what it took to persuade you of my sincerity."

She chuckled. "Wow."

"In fact, I may do it anyway." With that, he kissed her.

When Christy finally came up for air, she scooted away. "Before we take this to its logical conclusion, I want everything perfectly clear between us. My cancer could return. Derek and Emma might never have a cousin or two. We could—"

"Whatever happens, I'm going into our relationship with both eyes open," he assured her. "Do I need to sign your list in blood or is my word good enough?"

She smiled. "Your word is enough," she said simply.

"Good. While we're tossing out worst-case scenarios, I could develop a life-threatening disease in five, ten or twenty years. I had mumps as a child and could be sterile. What if I walk into the hospital parking lot and a runaway car runs me down? Could you deal with *my* issues if they ever happen?"

His points made her realize she might be making more out of her worries than necessary. "Yes. However, there's one more thing for you to consider."

"Christy," he said kindly, "whatever your concern, it isn't as important as you think it might be. I love you for the woman you are."

"That's sweet of you to say, but I want to give you one last chance to change your mind. You may not need to see this, but I need to show you."

She led him into her bedroom and turned her back toward him. "Unzip me, please. I can't reach."

"This is completely unnecessary."

"I don't agree. Just do it."

As soon as he tugged down the zipper, she turned around to face him. Slowly, carefully, she let the gown drop to the floor.

"I want you to see exactly what you're getting," she said softly. "If you're repulsed—"

She held her breath and watched his expression as he gazed at her manmade curves. She saw interest and awe, but not disgust, and she finally allowed herself to breathe.

He traced her collarbone with a feather-light touch before trailing his fingers down her breastbone. Meeting her gaze without flinching or hesitation, he suddenly pulled her against his chest and covered her back with his hands.

"I see the most beautiful woman in the world."

Although logic said otherwise, she was thrilled he thought so. "Will you stay with me tonight?"

He nodded. "On two conditions."

She raised an eyebrow. "And they are?"

"One, I won't leave until morning. In fact, I won't leave until it's time for our flight."

Surprised by his comment, she asked, "Do you want to come along?"

"Nothing could keep me away. In fact, I bought my ticket two weeks ago. I had planned to go with you, one way or another."

If she'd needed final proof that he would stick by her, no matter what, he'd just provided it.

"What's the second condition?"

"That you agree to marry me. I want you to know beyond all doubt that I won't be influenced by the outcome of your appointment."

Although she'd suspected as much, until now she'd been afraid to believe. "I know you will," she said simply. "And, yes, I'll be your wife."

His grin instantly stretched across his face be-fore he stepped back and began unbuttoning his shirt. "Good. Now that we've addressed those minor details, I want to make love with you."

She wanted to cry with happiness and all she could do was nod her agreement.

"I hope you got a nap this afternoon," he added, "because we won't be sleeping most of the night."

Christy helped with his buttons, enjoying the feel of his hard chest beneath her fingers. "Is that so?"

"Oh, yes," he assured her, before he stepped out of his trousers and drew her against him once again. "It's a promise."

Christy sat in her oncologist's private office with Linc beside her as they waited for Dr Kingston to walk in. He'd conducted his exam in his usual noncommittal manner and after he'd finished, he'd suggested she join him in his office as soon as she'd dressed.

She pulled on her clothes in record time.

As she sat in front of the doctor's desk, outwardly she was calm, but inwardly she was a bundle of nerves.

"Whatever he tells us, we'll deal with it," Linc assured her as he held her hand in his strong one.

She managed a smile. "I know, but—"

"Think optimistically," Linc told her.

The door swung wide and Dr Kingston entered. He was tall, thin, and reminded her of an oversized scarecrow, but his eyes were full of compassion. He also seemed older than she remembered, but she supposed his job was more difficult and more stressful than most.

"Sorry for the delay," he said in a kindly voice that matched his expression. "I had to take a phone call."

Christy introduced Linc, then waited for the oncologist to open her chart on his desk.

"You're doing well?" he asked. "Still enjoying your job?"

"Oh, yes."

"My wife insists I need to take a vacation. Maybe we should travel to the Midwest. I haven't been in the area in years."

"It's a wonderful part of the country," she agreed, fighting her impatience.

"I imagine it is. But, then, you aren't here to listen to my vacation plans, are you?" Without waiting for her response—which was a good thing because she suddenly couldn't breathe—he opened her folder. "Ah, yes. I remember now. Your results came in a week ago."

"And?" she asked, her palms suddenly moist.

He leaned back in his chair and steepled his fingers. "Your scans are clear. No sign of any abnormalities."

Christy's shoulders slumped and tears came to her eyes as Linc hugged her.

"Your tumor marker levels haven't changed either, so I'd say you passed your five-year checkup with flying colors."

"Thank you," she choked out.

He smiled. "I'll be happy to take the credit because I don't often have the opportunity to deliver good news. Out of curiosity, though, I know you celebrate your anniversary with an adventure. What did you plan for this year?"

Christy looked at Linc and smiled at him with all the love in her heart. "A wedding."

* * * * *

Mills & Boon® Large Print Medical

January

SYDNEY HARBOUR HOSPITAL: MARCO'S TEMPTATION	Fiona McArthur
WAKING UP WITH HIS RUNAWAY BRIDE	Louisa George
THE LEGENDARY PLAYBOY SURGEON	Alison Roberts
FALLING FOR HER IMPOSSIBLE BOSS	Alison Roberts
LETTING GO WITH DR RODRIGUEZ	Fiona Lowe
DR TALL, DARK...AND DANGEROUS?	Lynne Marshall

February

SYDNEY HARBOUR HOSPITAL: AVA'S RE-AWAKENING	Carol Marinelli
HOW TO MEND A BROKEN HEART	Amy Andrews
FALLING FOR DR FEARLESS	Lucy Clark
THE NURSE HE SHOULDN'T NOTICE	Susan Carlisle
EVERY BOY'S DREAM DAD	Sue MacKay
RETURN OF THE REBEL SURGEON	Connie Cox

March

HER MOTHERHOOD WISH	Anne Fraser
A BOND BETWEEN STRANGERS	Scarlet Wilson
ONCE A PLAYBOY...	Kate Hardy
CHALLENGING THE NURSE'S RULES	Janice Lynn
THE SHEIKH AND THE SURROGATE MUM	Meredith Webber
TAMED BY HER BROODING BOSS	Joanna Neil

Mills & Boon® Large Print Medical

April

A SOCIALITE'S CHRISTMAS WISH	Lucy Clark
REDEEMING DR RICCARDI	Leah Martyn
THE FAMILY WHO MADE HIM WHOLE	Jennifer Taylor
THE DOCTOR MEETS HER MATCH	Annie Claydon
THE DOCTOR'S LOST-AND-FOUND HEART	Dianne Drake
THE MAN WHO WOULDN'T MARRY	Tina Beckett

May

MAYBE THIS CHRISTMAS…?	Alison Roberts
A DOCTOR, A FLING & A WEDDING RING	Fiona McArthur
DR CHANDLER'S SLEEPING BEAUTY	Melanie Milburne
HER CHRISTMAS EVE DIAMOND	Scarlet Wilson
NEWBORN BABY FOR CHRISTMAS	Fiona Lowe
THE WAR HERO'S LOCKED-AWAY HEART	Louisa George

June

FROM CHRISTMAS TO ETERNITY	Caroline Anderson
HER LITTLE SPANISH SECRET	Laura Iding
CHRISTMAS WITH DR DELICIOUS	Sue MacKay
ONE NIGHT THAT CHANGED EVERYTHING	Tina Beckett
CHRISTMAS WHERE SHE BELONGS	Meredith Webber
HIS BRIDE IN PARADISE	Joanna Neil